DEADLY SIOUX

A HUCK CLEMONS WESTERN - BOOK TWO

SCOTT HARRIS

PRODUCTIONS

1

THE RETURN

Sophie was the first one to notice the wagons rolling down the gently sloping hill toward the ranch. She shaded her eyes against the brilliant morning sun and pulled her coat closed against the chill, trying to figure out who was heading toward the homestead.

Because she was only expecting one wagon and didn't recognize the first two men she saw riding horseback, it took her a moment to realize what she was seeing. When she did, she let out a yell that brought everyone racing from the main house and the bunkhouse, many of the men with rifles in hand.

Brock was the first one to reach her and he looked where she was pointing, instantly recognizing the Circle CM wagon, but like Sophie, confused about much of what he saw. What he did know was that the wagons presented no threat, so he made sure the men put away their weapons as he started walking toward the wagons. Sophie joined him, as did their daughter, Annabelle.

As they drew closer, things became clearer. While they didn't know two of the three riders, they saw that the third was Tom James, Huck's best friend since childhood. Brock could see he was hurting, though he couldn't tell if it was illness or injury.

At the same time, Sophie and Brock saw their son, Huck, sitting up front on one of the wagons and noticed the beautiful young woman sitting next to him with the reins in her hand. They both assumed she was Sarah, Huck's fiancée. Picking her up in Abilene and moving her here was the reason that Huck, Tom and Kentaki, his Havasupai Indian friend, had left three months ago. They had no idea who the woman was in the second wagon, though she appeared to be pretty comfortable with the reins.

Brock took a quick look and realized that Kentaki was not riding or in either wagon. He hoped that meant he'd returned to his home in the Grand Canyon and that nothing had happened to him. Annabelle, having spotted her brother, raced ahead of her parents—to her favorite person on Earth—and leapt into the wagon. Brock saw Huck wince as she did and knew something was wrong with him, as well as with Tom.

Before he could say anything, the biggest surprise of all happened. Maria Hinojosa popped up her head from the back of the wagon. Sophie started to smile but saw that Maria's face was covered with tears. Maria was Sophie's closest friend, but she, her husband, Cisco, and their son, Enyeto, had decided a few months previously to leave the ranch and move back home to Tesuque in New Mexico Territory. She knew the tears were not ones of joy.

Sophie and Brock were joined by Ray, Sophie's father, and Pukeheh, Ray's Havasupai wife. The wagons rolled to a stop and things quickly became hectic and confusing.

Annabelle couldn't understand why Huck hadn't jumped off the wagon to greet her, and Sophie's attention turned to her obviously troubled friend. As hard as it was to rush straight past Huck to Maria, she did. She went around the back of the wagon and two terrible things registered at once. Cisco was lying in the wagon, struggling to sit up and obviously hurt. And worse, she did not see Enyeto.

Brock went to his son and helped him down from the wagon, once he'd peeled Annabelle away. He could see it was the leg that was hurting him. Before he could say anything, Huck spoke.

"The leg's nothing. Same with Tom's shoulder. Cisco's hurt the worse. But, Dad, Enyeto... Enyeto was killed. He and Cisco were out riding, their horse hit a hole and crashed. Enyeto, he was tossed clear, but his neck..."

Brock wrapped his son in his arms, thankful he was alive and safe, but devastated by the news that was pouring out. He asked, "The leg?"

"Gunshot, but it'll be okay with some time. Same with Tom. Took a bullet in his shoulder. Let's get Cisco out of this wagon and into a bed, and I'll tell you all about everything."

Brock started to move toward the back of the wagon when Huck stopped him. He reached up and took Sarah's hand and helped her from the wagon, saying, "This is Sarah Huckaby, my fiancée. Sarah, this is my father, Brock Clemons."

Sarah did a little curtsey, smiled and said, "It is a pleasure to meet you, Mr. Clemons."

In spite of everything he had learned in the last two minutes, Brock laughed. "Young lady, as I understand it, you're going to be marrying my son. It may be a little early for you to be comfortable calling me Dad, but how about we start with Brock?"

Just then, one of the two men Brock didn't know rode up and dismounted. "Mr. Clemons, my name's Jimmy Huckaby. This young woman here is my daughter. It's a pleasure to meet you."

"It's Brock, and it's a pleasure to meet you, too. I look forward to our sitting and talking, but it sounds like there's been some trouble and some people need lookin' after?"

"There has been and they do. We've done what we can, but none of us are doctors." As he finished, Ray and Pukeheh walked up and Brock turned toward them.

"Mr. Huckaby, this here is Pukeheh. She is a medicine

woman from the Havasupai tribe. Comes from the Grand Canyon. Married Sophie's dad. Nobody better with sickness or injury. Huck said Cisco needs care first?"

"He does. If you've got a bed, how 'bout I help you and we carry him in?"

Pukeheh spoke. "Please bring him into the main house. I'll get a bed ready. Ray, come help me get ready. We'll have time later for everyone else." Ray did as he was told.

Brock immediately liked Jimmy Huckaby, how he was respectful, but didn't hesitate to offer suggestions and help. They walked to the back of the wagon and were joined by the other man he didn't know.

As the third man helped with Cisco, Jimmy said, "Brock, this is Harry Wheeler, former sheriff of Abilene and a friend of mine. The woman you haven't met yet is my fiancée. I'm guessing you weren't expecting any of us, but I'm hoping there's room our here for us to make a new life."

2

INTRODUCTIONS

Pukeheh took control of the medical needs, while Sophie started to take care of everything else. As the men carried Cisco into the main house, Sophie directed them to the largest of the extra bedrooms. Maria objected.

"Sophie, we can't..."

"Maria, you better not say impose. You and Cisco will stay here as long as you need. As long as you want. You have to know that you are family and we'll do whatever we can, whatever you need."

Maria simply reached across and gave Sophie a bear hug as the three men made sure Cisco was as comfortable as possible in the bed. Pukeheh followed the men in, ordering them out as she did, even before Brock could say anything more to his friend than 'hello.' Sophie followed as well, needing to hold her son and to make sure everything was organized. Maria and Pukeheh remained in the room with Cisco, and Pukeheh started attending to the leg.

Waiting in the main room were Tom, Huck, the two men Sophie didn't know and the two women, one of whom she knew was Sarah, though they hadn't been introduced. Without a word, she walked straight to Huck and wrapped her arms around him. Huck was unsure if she would ever let go. When she finally did, Huck dropped into the closest chair and Sophie noticed for the first time that something was wrong with his leg. She gasped and Huck said, "I'll be fine. I just need to rest the leg, but I'll be fine. Tom will too."

"Tom? What happened to you?"

"I got nicked in the shoulder, but I really am fine, better than Huck."

Harry Wheeler who had been standing in the corner, stepped forward and spoke. "Ma'am, my name's Harry Wheeler. We haven't been introduced, but about all Huck has talked about for over a thousand miles on the trail has been his family. Unless I miss my mark completely, you must be Huck's mother, Sophie."

"I am."

"And the beautiful young lady standing next to you? That must be Annabelle. According to Huck, she's the prettiest, smartest and toughest young gal in the West."

No one had ever seen Annabelle blush before, but she did now and it brought a smile to everyone's faces. Harry continued, "You, sir, must be Ray, Sophie's father and Huck's grandfather. Huck says Annabelle gets her toughness from you and from her mother. That about right?"

Ray and Sophie nodded and Harry kept going. "Allow me to introduce the people you've so generously invited into your home. As I said, I'm Harry Wheeler. Was sheriff in Abilene until I caught up with this idea of heading north with everyone else. I know no one here was expecting me, so I hope it's okay. Heard you're building a new town and I'd like to be a part of it. Anything but sheriff."

Sophie, her mind reeling, simply answered, "Of course."

Harry continued with the introductions, pointing to Jimmy. "This man is Jimmy Huckaby. Owned a restaurant in Abilene, but more important to this conversation, he's Sarah's father. The woman standing next to him is Madeline Stawarski, though we all call her Maddie. She's hitched her wagon to Jimmy here, though I think it's fair to say she thought that wagon was destined to stay in Abilene. And last, and certainly most important, ah hell, Jimmy..."

Jimmy Huckaby smiled and walked over to stand next to Sarah. "You've already figured it out, but this is my little girl. Sarah Marie Huckaby. I guess soon to be Sarah Clemons. Brock, I see you've got a beautiful and smart daughter—"

Brock interrupted and said, "Yes, but she's only..."

Jimmy stopped him and said, "Sooner than you can

possibly imagine, you're gonna be standing in front of some folks, hoping to God they're good people and that they raised a good son. I've gotten to know your Huck while we were on the trail and I can't imagine a better man for my Sarah to marry. Makes it easier it does, but it's still tough."

Sophie took two steps forward and took Sarah's hand in hers. "Sarah, I am so sorry there is so much happening here today, some of it terrible. But please know how excited Brock and I are to meet you and how much we're looking forward to you being a part of our family. You're all Huck could talk about from the time he first met you until he left to pick you up Abilene. You are every bit as pretty as Huck said you are, and I am so much looking forward to our getting to know you."

As Sophie finished, Pukeheh walked out of the bedroom and into the main room. She looked at Tom and said, "Off with your shirt, Tom. Let's see what we're looking at."

Tom started to object, but Ray stopped him. "Young man, you know you're gonna wind up doing what she says. Now, off with the shirt and let her see about that shoulder. Huck, you'll be next."

Tom, thinking about how Huck would have to remove his pants for Pukeheh to look at his leg, started to laugh. Huck didn't join him. Pukeheh turned to Ray and Annabelle. "Bring me some hot water and clean cloths. Some of that salve I like to use, too."

Sophie turned back to her guests. "Cisco and Maria will stay here. Miss Maddie and Miss Sarah, if you don't mind sharing a bedroom, you can stay at the main house, too. Mr. Huckaby. Mr. Wheeler, you'll stay at Huck's house with him and Tom. Once everyone's healthy and wedding plans have been made, we'll look at where everyone will stay permanently, but this will work well for now.

"We have a couple of hours before the evening meal. Maybe everyone can get unpacked and cleaned up. Maybe even rest a little before we gather."

Sophie could not have been more surprised—or more pleased—than when Sarah stepped forward and, without a word, reached out and hugged her.

3

SUPPER

It was a very large group that gathered two hours later for supper. It was so large that the guests spilled from the dining room into the main room. Cisco remained in his bedroom as Pukeheh insisted he needed his rest and that he had to stay in bed for at least a week—though she shared that he would make a full recovery.

Everyone else who'd ridden in that day—Tom, Huck, Sarah, Jimmy, Maddie, Harry and Maria—were in the dining room, along with Sophie, Brock, Annabelle, Ray and Pukeheh. They were also joined by Huck's little brother, Levi, who'd grown so much just since Huck had left for Abilene that he couldn't believe it.

Pukeheh announced that after cleaning Huck and Tom's wounds and covering them with fresh bandages that both would make full recoveries. They just needed a little time. She planned to keep a close eye on both to make sure they allowed themselves to get healthy again.

The dining room was filled with people who had become a part of the Clemons family over the years. Sitting at the head of the table was Gus Seldon. Huck had found and hired Gus in Abilene the previous year to buy a herd of cattle—a large herd with two thousand head of the finest cattle available—and then bring that herd from Abilene to the Circle CM.

At the other end of the table was Dario Serna. The Clemons family had met Dario when they lived in the Grand Canyon with the Havasupai. Dario had run a general store, Dario's Mercantile, in Hardyville and decided to give up life on the Colorado River for whatever adventures he would find traveling with the Clemons family. He had found plenty. Since Ray had owned a general store in Dry Springs, the town in Colorado Territory where Sophie was born and raised, the two of them had become fast friends.

Sitting on either side of Dario were Alex Ball and Kevin Calderwood. Kevin was known previously as Major Kevin Calderwood and he ran Fort Mojave, which was located about twenty miles from Hardyville. Brock and Huck had brought two killers, men who had slaughtered defenseless Hopi Indians, including a woman and her infant son, to be tried at the fort.

The man who tried them was known back then as Circuit Court Judge A.F. Ball. He was now known simply as Alex. Alex and Kevin, along with Dario, had decided that they wanted new challenges, new lives, and as so often happened, they were attracted to Brock and the life he led. They'd all been together ever since.

Also at the table was Claude Pierre, a French trapper and trader who had introduced himself to the men of the Circle CM when they were in Casper, still bringing the cattle north. He convinced them he knew the trails, the lay of the land, and the way of the Indians, and rode with them from Casper to the ranch. Like so many, he'd stayed and looked forward to starting a new life in the town that was to be built. Claude Pierre had only one leg, but it was easy not to notice as he moved well and did as much work as any of the other men.

The last two in the main room were Willy and Ten. They had been stagecoach drivers for years and had a reputation as being the best in the West. They were hired by people who had valuable items, or valuable people, to move. They'd been shot at more times than either could remember. Willy had finally convinced Ten that even their good fortune could run out, and it was time to find a new line of work.

Ten, whose name came from the ten-gauge shotgun he carried almost everywhere, reluctantly agreed. They had run into Huck more than once on the trails over the past couple of years, the last time as they were being chased by a large group of very persistent outlaws. The outlaws were killed, friendships forged and Willy and Ten, like so many others, found themselves with their wagons hitched to the Circle CM, Brock and Sophie.

All told, twenty-one people sat down for supper. Huck looked around the room, once again marveling at the people in his life and the large variety of ways in which they got there. As he was thinking about it, Brock stood up and after a minute or two, was able to quiet everyone down. When he had their attention, he raised his glass and the others all followed.

He started, "Sophie and I want to welcome all of you to our home. By the looks of it, we should have built a bigger place, but I see we all squeezed in."

There was some easy laughter and Brock continued, "Some of you are family, some are long-time friends, and some are brand new friends. But I hope that each and every one of you either considers yourself, or soon will, a part of the Circle CM family. We all have stories to tell, stories to hear, hopes and dreams to share. We need to figure out so many things and there is plenty of planning and plenty of work ahead of us. We have both a ranch and a town to build and neither will be easy.

"But let's leave all of that for tomorrow. For tonight, let's enjoy our meal, each other's company and begin to get to know one another. But before we do, there is one more thing I want to say."

Brock stopped and looked at Maria and then continued. As he did, Sophie stood and joined him.

"I mentioned family before. It is not a word I use lightly. I left London a number of years ago and when I did, I left my family behind. I have not been home since. I share this because Cisco and Maria Hinojosa are family to Sophie and me. I met Cisco in the middle of a small gun battle that we barely escaped. Neither of us would have made it without the other. A man was killed in that battle and though I didn't know him, I know he was a good man.

"I know this because he convinced Maria to marry him, something only a good man could have done. P'oe and Cisco were the best of friends and when P'oe was killed, Cisco began to care for Maria, including her and P'oe's son, Enyeto, a child he was never able to meet.

"Cisco married Maria and raised Enyeto as his own. Cisco and Maria became Sophie's and my closest friends. It saddened us when they decided to move back to New Mexico Territory, but we understood. Sadly, incredibly sadly, tragedy struck. As you all know, little Enyeto was killed. It was no one's fault, but unfortunately, sometimes, these things happen.

"For those who knew Enyeto, you knew how special he was. He brought joy everywhere he went. He was filled with curiosity and life and brought smiles to all of us. His loss is a terrible thing. None of knows what the future holds. Cisco and Maria have another child on the way, and we are all praying for the best.

"But for tonight, I would like to toast little Enyeto. For the young boy he was, for the life and laughter he brought to all who knew him, and to his parents, Cisco and Maria, who could not have loved him more.

"To Enyeto!"

4

SUNRISE

The following morning, Huck was up before dawn and before Jimmy, Harry or Tom. It didn't take much to get the fire going. As soon as there was hot coffee available, Huck poured himself a cup and stepped outside onto the front porch.

It was cold and Huck's jacket was buttoned to the top and he covered the rest of his neck with a scarf Annabelle had given him for Christmas. He settled into one of the four rocking chairs he kept on the porch. His house was only a hundred yards or so from the main house, and he could easily see it from where he sat. It sat atop a small knoll, just high enough to give them a fantastic view of everything that surrounded the house.

The bunkhouse was behind the main house and out of view, but he could see the stables. The horses were starting

to move, ready for someone to emerge from the bunkhouse
and give them some hay and grain. He could see the small
house, some might call it a cabin, that had been built for
Ray and Pukeheh. They knew they were welcome to live
with Sophie and Brock in the main house and while they
still planned on eating most of their meals there, they
wanted a little privacy.

To Huck's right, the small foothills grew into mountains
and there was still snow on the highest points. The as yet
unnamed creek meandered down from the mountains, ran
behind Huck's house and filled the pond in the middle of
the large pasture.

That pasture sat to Huck's left and held the two thousand head of cattle they'd driven up from Abilene. The
animals weren't fenced in, but still stayed close. They had
fresh water, plenty of sweet grass, and Huck guessed that
on some level, they knew the things living in the large
boxes would protect them from grizzlies, wolves and
rustlers. It made it easier on the ranch hands having them
stay so close, so docile, so well-watered and so easily fed.

Huck watched as a coyote patrolled the outside of the
pasture, but finding no calves and no weakened cows, it
kept going. Because it did, Huck felt no need to use the
Remington 1858 he kept next to him. The coyote, not
knowing how close it had come to death, kept trotting. A
half dozen elk came down from the hills, sipped from the
creek and kept going, though in the opposite direction of

the coyote. Hawks circled in the sky and squirrels were just starting to chatter at each other and anything else they saw.

Huck's leg ached, but he knew it would get better. He just needed a little rest and a little time. He saw smoke from behind the main house and knew one or more of the ranch hands had started their day with a fire and some hot coffee. Huck knew there was a rhythm to the mornings, and he looked forward to staying here long enough to join them. There is a comfort to that, one Huck hadn't had in a while.

Just as he could start to see the bottom of his cup, the front door opened and Tom walked out, with a hot cup in each hand. He handed one to Huck and sat down in one of the open chairs.

"How long you been out here?"

"No more than a half hour. Long enough to see the sun start her day, but not much more than that. How's the shoulder?"

"Whatever Pukeheh put on it made all the difference. I can move it around more than I've been able to."

"You know she said to take it easy for a while."

"I know, but it ain't easy."

"Nope, guess it ain't."

Huck looked across at his friend and asked, "Guessing you'll be heading to the Square M soon?"

The Square M was the second largest ranch in Montana Territory, after the massive Grant-Kohrs ranch. It was owned by Katie Warner. Katie was a strong woman and reminded Huck—and anyone else who knew both of them —of Sophie. Sophie and Katie had become fast friends and since the ranches shared a border, he knew they'd be able to help each other out when needed.

As Huck knew, a more immediate concern to Tom was Katie's younger sister, Claire. She had come out to her sister's ranch at about the same time everyone from the Circle CM had arrived. She'd arrived escorted by a Warner family friend, Walt Butler. Walt was closing in on seventy years old and had lost his left arm years ago. He stood ramrod straight and a full eight inches over six feet. Seventy or not, it would take a brave man to tangle with Walt.

Clair was a year older than Tom and a beautiful young woman. Tom was smitten with her immediately and she knew it, in the way beautiful women do. It was equally clear to everyone (except Tom) that she had an eye for him, confirmed when she announced just before Huck and Tom had left for Abilene that she intended to make her visit permanent.

Tom wanted to tell Huck it was none of his business and maybe even pretend he didn't have feelings for Claire, but he knew that was a waste of time.

"Let's say I do ride over there. What'm I gonna say? What if she doesn't feel the same way 'bout me, that her wanting to stay had nothing to do with me?"

"Tom, I'm not saying I know women well. I'm still not sure how I was able to win Sarah's hand, but before we left, I heard Katie and my mother talking about it and they both think she has her heart set on you. You think they don't know?"

"You didn't tell me that! All the way to Abilene and back and you didn't say a word. Why?"

"Well, Tom, you said you didn't have feelings for Miss Claire."

"But you knew..."

"I did. I do. I also know there was nothing you coulda done while we were on the trail and frankly, I was having a little fun with you. I'm letting you know now so you don't do anything stupid, like not riding over there today and inviting her, Katie and Walt for supper this week."

"Huck, you son of a—"

"Now, Tom, you wanna stay out here and fight with me, or maybe get yourself cleaned up and ride over to the Square M?"

Tom was still mumbling curses and threats when he walked back inside the house to do exactly what Huck had suggested.

5

PLANS

Huck stepped back into the house to find that Jimmy and Harry were both awake, both with a cup of coffee in their hands. Tom was getting a few things together for his ride to the Square M, bringing enough to make the round trip in a day, or to be able to stay the night, if invited.

Jimmy spoke first. "Morning, Huck."

"Good morning, Jimmy. Sleep well?"

"I did. Been thinking since we got here. No, I guess since before we got here, but staying in this house makes it come to mind quicker."

Huck didn't say anything. He took a seat and waited for Jimmy to continue. He did. "We're both planning on gettin' married, right?"

"Yessir."

"All we ever said was, 'When we get to Montana,' right?"

"Yessir. That's been the plan."

"Well, we're here now. We're in Montana."

"We are, but I'm not followin' you."

"Guess I'm just wondering, since we're here now, when you plan on marrying my daughter? Follows then I gotta figure out when Maddie and me are gonna get hitched too. Don't think I wanna wait too long. You?"

It hit Huck that he hadn't really thought about that. Jimmy was right; the plan was to get married once they reached the ranch. Huck always figured they'd talk more about it as they drew close. But with Cisco and Enyeto's accident, then he and Tom getting shot, the focus became surviving and the conversation never happened. But they were here now.

All three of the injured men were going to recover. Huck's house was built. Sure, there was some more furniture to buy and some decorating to do, but that was no reason to hold off on getting married. Truth was, he couldn't think of a reason to hold off. Surprising himself, as well as Jimmy and Harry, Huck sprung from his chair—at least as quickly as he could with the bad leg—and said, "You're right. I'm gonna go talk to Sarah right now. No reason to wait."

Jimmy, surprised, said, "Hold on. I didn't say it had to be today."

"No, sir. You were right. No reason to wait. Been waitin' long enough."

And with that, he turned and walked out the front door. Jimmy and Harry watched as he headed toward the main house. Harry looked at his friend and said, "What the hell... What just happened?"

"I think my little girl is going to be getting married here right quick."

This time Harry laughed as he said, "You know what that means, don't ya?"

"Well, I already agreed to the wedding and came all the way up here, so I guess sooner is good."

"No, Jimmy. Means you better get to talking to Maddie. Huck and Sarah make any plans today and you haven't talked to Maddie, she ain't gonna be happy. No woman would. She came just as far and after traveling all the way from Pittsburgh before she even got to Abilene. She's more than ten years older than your Sarah. If it was me, I'd go running right past that young man 'fore he makes you look bad."

"Ah, hell, Harry, I been so focused on my Sarah, guess I haven't been as good to Maddie as I should be. Thing is, maybe it's best Huck talks to Sarah and once we know what they're doing, me and Maddie can make our plans."

Huck reached the front door of the main house and let himself in. He found Sophie, Huck, Maddie, Ray and Sarah sitting around the dining room table with coffee and tea.

Ray spoke first. "Morning, Huck. Pukeheh and Maria are in checking on Cisco. Heard him say it was the best night sleep he'd had since the accident."

"That's good news. Tom said he's feeling much better too. Whatever salve Pukeheh gave him is working magic. Me? I was able to walk over here and at a pretty good pace, I might add." He remained standing until Sarah waved him to the open chair next to her. He sat and asked, "How did you sleep?"

"The best I have in a long time. I think the cool weather works for me."

"Sarah, I'd like to marry you."

She laughed as the others looked on, obviously confused. "In case you forgot, I already said yes. Even rode over a thousand miles just to be here with you."

Looking slightly embarrassed, Huck pushed forward. "Yes. Yes, you did and I haven't forgotten. What I meant was, I want to marry you right away. This Saturday."

Sophie jumped in. "Huck, that's only a week from now. That's not enough time to plan a wedding."

Huck looked at Sophie. "If I remember right, that's about how long it was from you saying yes to Brock until the wedding, and that's seemed to work pretty darn well."

Sophie started to answer, but instead Sarah did. "Yes." Huck turned to her. "Yes?"

"Yes, I'll marry you, and yes, I'll marry you Saturday."

Sophie, her mind racing said, "How can we—"

Brock stopped her. "Honey, Huck's right. No reason to wait, and I agree, it worked pretty well for us. Everyone who will be coming to the wedding lives right here anyway. We can certainly pull together everything we need."

Just then, Alex Ball walked in the front door. "I heard the talk as I walked up the steps. I can perform the wedding, if you'd allow me. 'Bout the only part of being a judge I enjoyed."

Brock smiled and added, "Huck, I've still got my good suit. You'd be welcome to wear it. I think you've grown into it."

"I'd be honored."

Sophie spoke next. "Sarah, I still have my wedding dress. If you'd like to wear that..."

"Thank you, Miss Sophie, but before we left Abilene, my father gave me my mother's wedding dress. It's packed with my things."

Just then Jimmy and Harry walked in the front door and could tell things were happening. Maddie surprised everyone when she turned toward Sophie and asked, "Forgive me for being so bold, but would it be possible for me to borrow your dress?"

"Of course!"

Maddie continued, "Sarah, I understand if you don't want..."

Sarah smiled and guessing what Maddie was going to say, said, "I think it would be perfect if you and my father got married this Saturday right alongside me and Huck. I can't think of anything better."

Jimmy, too stunned to speak, slowly lowered himself into one of the chairs.

"What the heck just happened?"

6

BEST MAN

Tom finished packing and walked across into the main house. Right away he could tell there was a lot more going on than just coffee. He looked around and started to ask, "What's happening..."

Sarah jumped up from her seat at the table and yelled, "Huck and I are gettin' married Saturday!" Before that could fully register, Maddie added, "Jimmy and I are too!"

Tom looked at his best friend, who looked extremely happy and then at Jimmy, who also looked happy, though maybe a little bit in shock.

Brock brought Tom up to date. "Huck and Sarah decided to get hitched on Saturday, and Maddie and Jimmy"—he stopped and looked at Jimmy, who still had a surprised and confused look on his face—"well, at least Maddie decided she and Jimmy would be too."

Tom looked around and asked, "This Saturday?"

Huck laughed and answered, "Yes and you better be back from the Square M by then, 'cause I expect you to be my best man."

Brock asked, "Square M?"

Huck laughed again and answered, "Yes, Tom is going to pay his respects to Miss Claire. But you will be back by Saturday, right?"

Tom, a bit embarrassed that everyone now knew why he was going to the Square M, nodded. He gathered himself enough to look at Sarah and Maddie. "Congratulations to you both. And yes, I fully intend to be back by Saturday, maybe even tomorrow. Heck, maybe today. I'm just riding over to... I wanted to... Aww, forget it! I'm just going."

As Tom turned and started to walk out, his face red and his mind racing with a variety of emotions, Harry spoke up. "Tom, if it's okay with you, I'd like to ride with you. Best I start to learn the territory and meet some of the neighbors. Hope you don't mind?"

Tom replied, "Not at all. I was gonna leave now, though."

Harry answered, "I'll be ready in ten minutes."

This time Jimmy jumped in. "Harry, you better be back before Saturday, since I expect you to be my best man."

Harry smiled, simply said, "I'd be honored," and left to start packing.

Sophie looked around the room as Pukeheh and Maria walked in. "Pukeheh, how's Cisco?"

"He's fine. Already stronger." Sophie took a minute and brought the two women up to date on what had happened the last few minutes. They both looked surprised and pleased.

Sarah said quietly, "Sophie, I know we only just met, but I was thinking that maybe, if you want to, you could, you could be my best maid Saturday? I know it's a little different, you being Huck's mom and all, but..."

"Sarah, I can't think of a better way to bring our family even closer together. I would very much like to be your best maid. There is a lot to do between now and Saturday, so we better get started right away."

As Sarah smiled with joy and relief, Maddie stood up and walked over to Maria. "Maria, we have not known each other very long, but after what we've been through together and the time we've spent on the trail, I was wondering if maybe..."

Maria took Maddie's hands and said, "I would love to."

Sophie, her skills as an organizer starting to kick in, looked at Brock. "We have a lot to do between now and Saturday. If a couple of men left today for Bozeman, could they be back by Saturday?"

"They could. Means they'll have to ride hard, but it can be done."

"Okay, I'll put together a list."

Less than thirty minutes later, Tom and Harry headed off to the Square M, hoping to be there by the mid-day meal. At the same time, brothers Jack and Jake Parker along with Jimmy Ray Johnson took off fast for Bozeman.

The three men were among the dozen cowboys that Gus had brought with him to bring the cattle from Abilene to the ranch. All twelve had decided to stay on and make new lives in Montana Territory. They had a large list of things that Sophie wanted for the wedding and instructions to ride hard to Bozeman, buy a wagon while they were there and head back as fast as they could with the supplies. With luck, they would be back by Friday.

FOUR HOURS LATER, after an uneventful ride, Harry and Tom rode into the front yard of the Square M's main house. The ride had been pleasant, as had the conversation, but now that they'd arrived, Tom was getting nervous and wondering if maybe he shouldn't have waited a bit before doing this. However, he was armed with an easy excuse, since he was now supposed to invited Katie, Walt and Claire to the weddings.

Before he could decide what to do next, the large double front door swung open and there stood Claire Warner, even more beautiful than Tom had remembered.

"Well, Mr. Tom James. This is how you treat a lady? Just show up unannounced and uninvited at her home?"

Tom, in shock and disappointment, struggled to get out any words and Claire could see right away that he was in trouble. "Tom, I was just kidding you. I am delighted that you are here and flatter myself to think that I might be at least part of the reason."

Finally finding the power of speech as Katie joined her sister on the porch, Tom stammered, "You are. Part of the reason. I planned to come here..."

Katie, taking pity on Tom, said, "Tom, why don't you climb down off your horse, introduce us to your friend, and step inside for something to eat and drink."

Tom looked around and saw that of the four people there, he was the only one who didn't find this whole thing funny. With a husky voice, he said, "Miss Katie, this is Harry Wheeler. He came with us from Abilene. He was the sheriff there but is now going to—"

Katie interrupted him. "Tom, dear, why don't we finish this conversation inside. Maybe some lemonade and a bite to eat will have you feeling more like yourself."

Two men who worked for Katie came over and took the horses from Tom and Harry. After handing over the reins, they walked toward the porch. It was all Claire could do to keep from laughing, but inside, she knew she was very happy to see Tom.

7

LOOKING BACK

Four hours later as they settled in for supper, Tom knew that he was hopelessly in love with Claire Warner. They had spent the afternoon on the porch, sipping lemonade and sharing stories, in the way people do when they really want to get to know each other.

Tom talked about growing up in Dry Springs and what it was like living in a small town in Colorado Territory. How Huck had been his best friend as far back as he could remember and how grateful he was for the life that Huck, Brock and Sophie had given him.

It wasn't that he didn't like Dry Springs; he did. But the idea of growing up to become a small town lawyer like his father had no appeal. It may have, before he left and saw other things, but no longer. Like Huck and Kentaki, once he'd been on the trail, he couldn't imagine going back.

Claire told him about her childhood. Her mother had died giving her life, and Walt and Katie had helped her father raise her. They were fortunate that they had money and a good life. She liked St. Louis and never imagined leaving.

"I only came out here for a visit. I missed my sister and all her letters made this place sound so beautiful. So different than anything I'd known. It's not that there isn't beauty in Missouri. There is. But it's different. There may be more people in St. Louis than in this entire territory. It is certainly different than anything I've ever seen."

Tom, growing fonder every minute, asked, "How long are you—I guess, you and Walt, going to stay? Before you go back to St. Louis, I mean."

"I'm not sure anymore. Just yesterday, Katie asked if we wanted to stay. Now that Daddy has died, we could sell the house, the property—we have a very nice farm just ten miles from the city—and maybe start a new life here. Katie certainly enjoys hers. Walt says he'll stay if I want to. Said at almost seventy years old, he doesn't relish another trip across the country, but it's up to me."

Tom's heart leapt into his throat. He asked, barely audible, "What did you tell her? What did you say to Miss Katie?"

Claire looked at Tom and waited for a moment before speaking. She smiled in a way that made his heart melt and his knees weak. Just as Tom almost asked again, fearing she hadn't heard his question, she answered, "I guess it depends on who else asks me to stay."

Before Tom could react, or even truly grasp what she was saying, she stood. As she started toward the door, she said, "I think I'll go take a rest now. I'll see you at supper?"

"Yes... I guess... Okay."

And she was gone, leaving Tom completely confused, hopeful, scared and excited.

JIMMY, Maddie, Brock, Sophie, Ray and Pukeheh sat down at the dining room table for supper. Maria was with Cisco, who continued to improve. Equally important to Sophie was that Maria seemed to be starting to recover as well, though she knew the pain of losing Enyeto would never go away.

The table was covered with elk stew, antelope steak, corn, potatoes, milk and tea. Jimmy had never had elk stew before and after his third bite, he said, "Not sure I've ever tasted anything like this before. This would have sold well in the restaurant."

Brock nodded and added, "Thing about a good stew is you can leave it over the fire for days. You can add things as they become available and the flavor just seems to get stronger and better with time."

Sophie laughed and said, "I think Brock would leave

that stew going forever. Can't do that myself. After a week or so, first day it seems to be getting low, I throw it out for the pigs. They love it and I get to clean the pot. Soon as it's clean though, Brock'll get a new stew going. Elk, beef, antelope, rabbit, doesn't matter. If it used to walk, he cuts it up and throws it in."

Brock added, "She's right. Not really a recipe you can write down, but something about that pot hanging over the fire just makes me feel good, 'specially come winter. Speaking of restaurants, Jimmy, have you figured out what you're gonna do now that you're here?"

Jimmy set his fork down next to the bowl of stew, looked at Maddie and answered, "Truth is, I haven't. It's a bit embarrassing to say, but I hadn't really thought it all the way through. I was so focused on Sarah, your Huck, winning Maddie's hand, selling the restaurant and getting here safely, I just didn't put any thought to what would happen once I got here."

Brock laughed and said, "I wouldn't worry about it none. There's plenty for you to do up here. Before me and Sophie started the CM, I was a sheriff in Dry Springs, a hunter in the Grand Canyon, an armed guard for a silver mine in California and ran sheep on a small island. I think this one is gonna take, but mostly because Sophie seems so happy here."

Maddie looked at Sophie. "Forgive me for asking, but are you?"

"Am I...?"

"Are you happy here? This is so different than anything I've ever known or even thought of, and well, I'm a little scared."

Sophie looked at Maddie and answered, "You should be scared. This is different than anything most of us have known, until we try it. We've been here less than a year, but I can't imagine ever living anywhere else. Like Brock said, we've tried a few things and most of them I enjoyed. But I never felt like this. We can build what we want, make of our lives what we want.

"There will be hard times. Already have been. But I think hard times come anywhere. I'm blessed that my family is here and there is so much beauty, so many things to do and huge opportunities. Yes, you're right, it's different. And yes, being a little scared is natural, but I wouldn't be anywhere else." She reached across and took Brock's hand. "Or with anyone else."

8

LOOKING FORWARD

Katie had a formal dining room and a second, smaller, more intimate one off to the side. The home was exquisite. Even to Tom's untrained eye, he could tell that a lot of time, thought and money had gone into building and decorating the home. He guessed that a lot of the furniture and other items he was looking at had been shipped here from Denver, San Francisco, or even St. Louis.

He appreciated being in the more casual dining room, as the main one was intimidating, with a hardwood table for twelve people, high-backed chairs and even a candle chandelier hanging from the high ceiling. This room had a lower ceiling, a rectangular table with seating for six, and the place settings were not so expensive as to make Tom nervous about eating off them.

However, the food could have been served at any table in the country. The main course, which was in front of them, was ring-necked pheasant. It was cooked in some sort of wine sauce that Katie explained but that Tom had barely heard. Just as he had barely touched the salad and rabbit livers that had come before the pheasant. His mind was on Claire and not much else.

Walt and Harry sat directly across from Tom, with Claire to his right and Katie to his left. Katie was dressed casually in what he had heard Sophie call a sun dress. She was certainly no less beautiful for the lack of formal attire. Tom sipped at the red wine that had been poured and prayed that he wouldn't do, or say, anything to embarrass himself, his mind still reeling from his conversation with Claire earlier.

Katie was kind enough to break the silence, saying, "Tell us about the wedding, Tom."

Tom looked up from his plate and at Katie, who was very nearly as beautiful as Claire. "It is actually two weddings. Huck is marrying Sarah. I think you know that's why we went to Abilene, to bring her back."

Katie answered, "Yes. We did know."

"Well, her father, Jimmy Huckaby, insisted on coming here too. Said his little girl wasn't going anywhere he wasn't gonna be. I don't know for sure, but I think Huck knew that before we got there. What we didn't know was that Mr. Huckaby had a met a woman from Pittsburgh, a teacher, name of Madeline Stawarski. Everyone calls her Maddie. They were planning on getting married too, so Maddie made the trip with us. You'll meet her when we get to the CM. And of course Harry here, he came too.

"Maddie said as along as Sarah didn't mind, she'd like to get married the same day. Everyone seemed to think it was a good idea and so now we're having two weddings come Saturday. Miss Sophie said it was important that you all come, since we're gonna be neighbors and friends."

"Of course, we'll be there, Tom. We wouldn't think of missing it. Claire, don't you agree?"

"I do. Mr. James, I believe I've been as clear as I can be about my feelings, but I remain a little confused as to your intentions. Did you ride all the way out here simply to invite the three of us to attend the festivities come Saturday, or was there another reason?"

Walt, Harry and Katie struggled to suppress smiles as Tom choked on his pheasant. He looked around desperate for help, but none was coming. Whatever was going to happen was up to him. Tom sensed the next minute or two could change his entire life. Finally, he found the strength to speak up. "Miss Claire, I'd like you to stay."

Claire was quite surprised, as were the others. Almost angrily, she asked, "You want me to stay home? Are you saying you would rather I did not come to the weddings?"

Whatever color red Tom's face had been, it was many

shades deeper now. He stammered a bit and finally got the words.

"No. No! I very much want you to come to the weddings. To be clear, I would like you to accompany me. I was answering you from this afternoon."

"What exactly are you answering?"

"This afternoon, on the porch, you said Miss Katie asked you to stay. You said you hadn't made up your mind yet, and it might depend on who else asked you to stay. Well, Miss Claire, I'm asking you to stay."

Claire smiled, reached across and took Tom's hand in hers and said, "Of course, I'm staying, Tom. I just needed you to ask."

BACK AT THE CM, the six were finishing up their own supper. Harry and Tom were gone, the three men had left for Bozeman, and the afternoon had been spent making wedding plans.

Dessert was two pies that Maddie had insisted on making. "I learned how to bake pies from my grandmother, my father's mother. My own mother never really did enjoy cooking, so I've still got a lot to learn. But if I do say so myself, Grandma knew how to bake cakes."

If the size of the bites and the speed with which the two pies disappeared were taken as commentary on the pies,

Maddie was right. Ray surprised everyone by having three pieces, one from the sour cherry pie and two pieces of the huckleberry pie. When he was done, he sat back in his chair, trying to be subtle about loosening his belt, which only served to get him smacked in the arm by Pukeheh. Then he turned to Jimmy.

"Pies like that could be the death of a man, Jimmy. Sophie's mom made a mean pie, but I don't think I ever ate three pieces at one sitting before. Going to have to be careful around Miss Maddie, that's for sure."

When the nods of agreement passed, Ray continued, "Jimmy. Maddie. Pukeheh and me been talking this afternoon. Don't mean to be too bold, but we were talking about you being here and what the future might hold. Jimmy, I know you said you didn't know yet what you wanted to do, so I was hoping you could help me out.

"I been asked to build the new town. I guess it's because I laid out our Dry Springs all those years ago, but things are different now. That was laid out for survival. This new town, well, we're all thinking one day it might be a decent-sized place, so we need to think about that now. We don't even have a name. I was hoping you might help me with the planning and overseeing the building. Going to be plenty to do, maybe too much for one man."

Jimmy looked around the table and saw that everyone was in agreement, including Maddie. "Ray, thank you for that. I think it makes a lot of sense. Give me something to do while me and Maddie figure out the future. Thing is, I gotta build us a place to live before I can help. Not sure if that works for you."

Ray looked at Pukeheh, back at Maddie and Jimmy, and smiled. "We talked about that too. We'd like you to live in our little cabin until you get settled. Plenty a room here in the main house for me and Pukeheh, and we like it here anyway."

Jimmy shook his head and started, "Ray, that's kind of ya, but we couldn't—"

Ray interrupted, "Jimmy, I respect you making decisions for your family, I really do. But do you think it's wise to tell my wife that you are declining her offer and then having to tell Miss Maddie that come Saturday night she's gonna be sleeping on the ground?"

Jimmy, knowing the truth when he heard it and knowing when he was beat, reached out and shook Ray's hand while Maddie stood up, walked over to Pukeheh and gave her a hug.

9

KENTAKI

As had become his habit, Huck was up before dawn, enjoying a cup of coffee on his front porch. Tom, Jimmy and Harry were still asleep, so Huck enjoyed the steam rising off the coffee—and the solitude.

The men who'd been sent to Bozeman had made the round trip in record time, returning Friday evening and bringing back the new wagon and all the supplies Sophie had ordered.

The preparations for the two weddings were proceeding without a glitch and Sophie seemed to Huck to be as excited about his wedding as Sarah was. He'd been excluded from most of the planning and felt relieved about that. He knew this was Sarah's day, or Sarah and Maddie's day, so whatever Sarah wanted was fine with him. All he knew was that starting tonight, she would be sharing his home, his bed and his life with him. There was nothing he could think of that he could want more than that.

Tom and Harry had returned from the Square M, along with Katie, Walt and Claire. It was obvious that Tom and Claire's relationship was advancing. Huck loved seeing his friend so happy, while at the same time, nervous as heck.

The only possible bad news was shared by Walt with Huck and Brock. On the ride over from the Square M, he had twice seen sets of tracks from what he thought were five riders. Neither the Square M nor the Circle CM had sent out groups of five riders in the past week, so they knew it wasn't them.

Added to the concern was the fact that the horses were unshod, almost guaranteeing they were Indians. They had no way of knowing which tribe, if they were simply traveling through or staying. And most importantly—whether they were friendly or not. Walt felt pretty certain they were warriors or hunters because there was no evidence of women or children travelling with them.

Brock told Gus so he could have the ranch hands be on alert, but they did not share it with the others so that the focus could remain on the weddings. Huck knew that the next day they would talk about it again and probably send men out to trail the five riders and try to figure out what their intentions were.

But for this morning, trusting that Gus was watching

things, Huck's thoughts were on the wedding and Sarah. He knew they had a lot of work to do to turn the house he'd built into a home, but Sarah was excited about doing it. Huck looked forward to watching the transformation.

He took a sip of the coffee as the sun just started to make itself known in the east. There was enough light that he could see the outline of the main house and look out over the main pasture at the cattle. Owls were giving their last calls for the night, merging nicely with the first calls from the roosters. A lone coyote was yipping on the back side of the hill and an easy fog was lifting.

As it did, Huck glimpsed a lone rider sitting on the top of the hill that overlooked both houses and the pasture. It was the same hill from where he'd first seen this land and the same hill where Sarah had taken her first look at her new home.

There was something familiar about the way the man sat on his horse, but even so, Huck picked up the rifle he always kept with him on the porch and set it across his lap. The man started to work his way down the hill, toward the house, clearly in no hurry or making any effort to hide himself.

As the rider drew closer, it was obvious he was bypassing the main house and heading straight for Huck and Sarah's home. Suddenly, Huck thought he knew who it was. He blinked his eyes a couple of times and then took another long look, not believing what he was seeing, but hopeful that he was right. As Huck stood up, the man waved and Huck knew.

It was Kentaki!

Huck set aside his rifle and walked down the stairs, meeting Kentaki as he dismounted. Without a word, the two men embraced.

"Kentaki. My goodness. How did you make it so fast? I am so happy to see you. Are you okay? How is Tochopa?"

Kentaki laughed, took a step back and answered, "I will tell you all, but maybe I could have a cup of coffee first?"

Huck said, "Of course," and went inside, returning to the porch with a hot cup of coffee and finding Kentaki in one of the rocking chairs. He hadn't noticed at first, but Kentaki looked very tired.

"My friend, are you okay? Are you hurt?"

"No, I am fine, though I am tired. When I woke yesterday at dawn, I saw five riders on a hill, maybe a mile away. I don't know who they were, but maybe Sioux. We have heard that some are coming this way and that they are not friendly. I don't know if they saw me, but I started riding and haven't stopped since. I saw no sign that they followed me, but I cannot be sure."

Huck shook his head. "Others have seen their trails. We have had no contact, but I believe Brock will take some of us tomorrow and go look for them. Best to find out right away if they are friendly or not. If they are, we can invite them in so that all who are friendly will know the Circle CM. If they are not, well…"

Kentaki nodded. "I will have slept by then and will join you for the search. But why tomorrow and not today?"

Just then the front door opened, Jimmy walked out, and answered for Huck,

"Huck and I are both gettin' married today. It's Kentaki, right?"

10

ALL FOR ONE

Kentaki stood up, though not without some effort, and shook hands as he said, "Good to see you, Mr. Huckaby. Did you say you're getting married too?"

"That I am, young man. Guess a couple of things have changed since I saw you last in Abilene. I know you were heading back to the Grand Canyon, then Huck said you were coming back this way."

Kentaki answered, "I guess that means you got the letter. Never sent one before. Good that it works. Man that took over for Dario is a good man. He must have understood what I wanted to say. At least most of it."

Just then Harry and Tom walked onto the porch. Tom dropped his coffee cup, splattering the coffee and breaking the cup all over the porch. "Kentaki!"

Kentaki reached out his hand, but Tom pulled him close with his good arm and gave him a hug, saying as he did, "Damn. It's good to see you. Huck said you were coming back, but I never expected to see you this soon."

"Rode hard and didn't have any problems. The hunting was good and plenty of water. Now, tell me about the wedding, or weddings?"

Huck looked at his friend, relieved that having made the long trip alone he had arrived safely. "Got to thinking there was no reason to wait. Sarah agreed and maybe most important, so did Mr. Huckaby."

"Jimmy. You gotta call me Jimmy."

"I try, I really do. But you being Sarah's father and all. Plus, I still can't get the meat cleaver out of my mind."

They all laughed and Jimmy said, "Okay, it'll come with time. As for me, you should have seen Maddie's face when Huck and Sarah decided to get married today. Wasn't nothing I could do to stop this from happening. Everyone's been helping out. Ray and Pukeheh even gave us their cabin, least until I can get one built. Not saying I didn't want to get married. I did, or I never would have dragged her all the way up here. Just not sure I saw it coming so quickly. Probably for the best. All these cowboys around here, she mighta changed her mind."

Huck leaned over and whispered something to Tom and though no one could hear, they all saw Tom smile and nod. Huck looked at Kentaki and said, "Now that you're here, I was wondering if you might, along with Tom, be my best man. I don't know if you have those in your marriage ceremonies, but to us, it's important."

Kentaki asked, "I don't know what that is, this 'best man,' but if you need me to be that, I will."

Huck smiled and answered, "When a man gets married, least when a white man gets married, his best friend stands with him at the altar. It's to offer support, though I heard it used to be a family member of the bride and his job was to make sure the groom didn't run away or change his mind.

"I promise you I won't be running anywhere and there's no chance I'll be changing my mind. I'd just like to have both of you"—he stopped and looked at Tom—"standing with me when I say yes."

Kentaki, looking very serious, said, "I will. Thank you, Huck. And thank you, Tom."

Harry noticed them first, but then they all saw Brock and Gus walking toward the house, each with their own cup of coffee. Huck stood and opened the front door, saying as he did, "I should have built a bigger porch. Tom, come help me grab some chairs."

Gus and Brock were thrilled that Kentaki had arrived safely, though both were concerned about the Indians he'd spotted less than a two days' ride from the ranch. Jimmy, Harry and Tom, who hadn't heard it yet from Walt or Kentaki, were told what had been seen.

Brock spoke next. "Enough of us know, we don't need to

be tellin' anyone else, especially the women. Today should be about the weddings. Gus' men know about it and they'll keep their eyes open for today. Come tomorrow, me and Gus will be heading out to see what we can find. Friendly or not, we need to know. A couple of boys from the bunkhouse'll riding with us."

So fast it sounded planned, Huck, Tom, Kentaki, Jimmy and Harry all said some version of 'Me, too.'

Brock looked at the men, knowing they all meant it, but also knowing everything else that was happening. "Harry, you can come along if you want. Be happy to have you with us. As for the others, appreciate it, but no."

Tom was the first to respond. "Why not? I know you own it, but this ranch is a part of all of us."

Brock looked at each man, letting his final gaze land on Tom. "Tom, I know that. Never questioned your loyalty or your courage, and you better know that by now. Things is, you're injured. Kentaki, you just rode in and you don't look like you could ride another mile. Huck, Jimmy, you're gettin' married tonight. How'd it look if the first morning after your wedding you were riding away?"

Huck looked hard at Brock and answered, "How'd it look if we didn't? You raised me to carry my weight. You told me just this week that once Sarah and I are married, my most important job is taking care of her. How's she gonna respect me? How'm I gonna respect myself if I let you ride off without me? No, I'll be riding with."

Jimmy looked around, his gaze landing on Brock. "Same here, Brock. I'll be mounted and ready when it's time to go. Man's gotta live with himself first. Didn't come all the way up here to hide behind your gun."

"Jimmy, I didn't mean..."

"I know you didn't, but let me make this easy on you. Would you stay?"

After only a moment's hesitation, Brock answered, "No. No, I guess I wouldn't. Kentaki, Tom, I'm not gonna talk you out of it either?"

Tom answered for both. "No, sir. I can ride, and I know I speak for Kentaki when I say it would take a lot more than a missed night's sleep to keep him from ridin' with us. Plus, you know he's the best tracker we got, even better than you or Gus."

Gus, who hadn't said a word, looked around at the men on the porch. "Well, hell, nobody I'd rather ride with than the men right here anyway. I'll make sure the ranch hands know to take care of the women and children first and double up on the watch. Jimmy, Huck, your new wives will need to move to the main house in the morning and stay 'til we get back. Make it easier to protect 'em.

"Now, we've got two weddings to finish getting ready for and come tomorrow, we leave at dawn."

11

WEDDING

Huck and Sarah stood before Alex Ball, Huck on the right with Tom and Kentaki by his side and Sarah, with Sophie by hers. He knew that seated behind him were both fathers, Ray and Pukeheh, and other family and friends. Annabelle, who had carried the ring once already today when Jimmy and Maddie got married had done the same thing for Huck and Sarah, though she refused to leave when she was done and was now standing beside him, holding his hand.

Huck listened as Alex went through the vows but having heard them less than a half hour ago, he allowed his mind to wander. He thought about Sarah and what it was going to be like being married to her, building their life together. If he was honest with himself, he was nervous about the wedding night, more nervous than he was about the next day when he'd be leaving his new bride to track down what he could only hope were friendly Indians.

But what he was really thinking about was Matt Lavender, known to all as Reverend Matt. Matt and his wife, Stacy, had moved to Dry Springs when Huck was thirteen. He had performed the ceremony for his parents' wedding on the same day they had adopted him. Huck had never known his mom; she'd died in childbirth, and his 'real' father had been killed while training a horse. Brock and Sophie had shocked him when they offered to adopt him. While he missed his father and the idea of his mother, he knew how incredibly fortunate he had been.

Matt and Stacy had been extremely close to his parents. Excluding Brock and Ray, Matt was the man Huck most admired in his life. In Dry Springs, Matt had helped build, and was then the reverend of, the Dry Springs Church of the Resurrection and was also the owner of the Dusty Rose, at the time the only saloon in Dry Springs. Huck always thought that Matt was the only man who could have done both, certainly at the same time.

Last year, when Huck had travelled to Abilene to buy the cattle, and as it turned out, to meet Sarah, Matt and Stacy had traveled in the other group with his parents as they made their way from Dry Springs to Montana Territory. Matt was shot in a gun battle with outlaws and eventually died from the wounds. Stacy never recovered from the death, eventually blaming it on Sophie and Brock. One day, she left the group for parts unknown.

She had not said goodbye, but left a terse, bitter note. They had not heard from her since. Huck knew that it still ate away at Sophie. He also knew there was nothing he could do for Stacy or his mother. And most of all, he knew how much he missed Reverend Matt.

His mind shifted back to the present when Annabelle dug her fingernails into his hand. He barely had time to focus before he heard Alex say, "Sarah, with an open heart and an open mind, knowing of the challenges you will face with the life you have chosen, do you choose Huck Clemons as the best man possible to share this life with?"

"I do."

"And Huck..."

"I do!"

There was some laughter from those watching. Huck, embarrassed at how he had jumped in, was relieved to see that Sarah had joined those who found his response funny.

Alex continued, "Sarah Huckaby and Huck Clemons, I now pronounce you married to each other and as of this day, will forever be known as Mr. and Mrs. Huckleberry Clemons. Huck, assuming Mr. Huckaby agrees, you may kiss the bride."

Huck heard Jimmy from his seat, with humor in his voice, answer Alex, "If you have to."

He did.

THE FOLLOWING MORNING, shortly before dawn, Huck woke his wife of less than twelve hours, wrapped her in a blanket and walked her from their home to the main house and straight to the bedroom she would be sharing with Maddie until the men returned.

Huck was so proud of his wife. After he'd explained to her why they had to track the Indians and why Huck felt so strongly that he needed to be among those who did, her protests stopped and she was fully supportive. Once again, Huck wondered about the life he'd brought her to, but once again, she assured him there was no place she would rather be.

After such a short period of time, it was hard for her to imagine any kind of life in Abilene that would satisfy her. While she had heard Huck, Tom and Kentaki talk about how their towns of Dry Springs and the Grand Canyon had become too small for them after what they'd seen during their travels, she thought now that Abilene was now too big for her. She decided it wasn't where any of them had left that mattered, but where they were and who they were with.

She kissed her husband goodbye, told him how much she loved him and put on a brave face. Just as Huck was leaving, she heard her father walk in with Maddie and was comforted that she would have someone with her, someone going through the exact same thing.

The seven men gathered in front of the main house. Each had three days' worth of food and water, but there was plenty of both where they were headed. They were all well-armed, with knives, pistols and rifles and plenty of ammunition. The decision was made that Kentaki, as the best tracker, would lead the way, but Brock would be in charge of all decisions. All the men knew that in situations like this, there needed to be someone in charge. Brock had been doing it for a long time. The fact that he was still alive meant he'd been doing it well.

The rode off in the direction that Kentaki had come. His sighting of the Indians was more recent than the tracks Walt had seen. While they hoped the tracks led away from the ranch, or at least were made by Indians friendly to white men and ranchers, none of them were confident that was the case.

SOPHIE KNOCKED GENTLY on the bedroom door, knowing Maddie and Sarah were on the other side and they couldn't possibly be asleep. She gently opened the door and asked both women to join her in the kitchen. When they arrived,

Maria and Pukeheh were already seated around the table, coffee was poured for all, and biscuits were heating up.

Nobody spoke as the women all sat.

12

FIRST DAY

The seven men rode in relative silence. Part of the quiet had to do with the amount of wine and bourbon drunk in celebration the night before. Part of it was that each man needed some time alone with their thoughts. Plenty was happening at the Circle CM. The men needed time to try and understand how it impacted them and, for those who had one, their families.

Huck's mind was on the beautiful young bride he'd left behind. Jimmy's thoughts, while slightly different, were along the same lines. Tom's thoughts had trouble with anything other than Claire. Harry, who thought he wanted a quieter life after Abilene was surprised at how much he was enjoying this, and Gus, for the first time, started to wonder how much longer he wanted to be chasing Indians into the wilderness, wondering if it might be time to turn the responsibilities for the ranch and the cattle over to another man.

Brock, whose mind never left the challenges in front of him, always felt most alive when he was on the trail. He wondered if he preferred it when he was alone, but he was certainly comforted having the quality of men surrounding him that he did.

Kentaki was focused on the trail and what clues any riders might have left behind. So far he had seen elk and antelope tracks and one set of good-sized grizzly prints, but no horses.

Harry broke the silence. "How ya feeling this morning, Jimmy? Like being married a second time?"

"Now, how could I possibly know that? Been married only a few hours and more of that spent chasing Indians than being with Maddie."

Harry smiled at his friend and turned toward Huck. "How 'bout you, Huck? And before you answer, don't forget her pa's right here."

Huck thought for a moment before answering, "Can't imagine anything better. Wish I was back there with her. 'Course I do. But I love this life. It may sound a little crazy, but doing this, doing what we're doing right now, I love it too. Truth is, me and Sarah, we been talking about what we're gonna do.

"Don't think I can live in a town, least not now. Too much to see everywhere else. On the other hand, I got a wife now and it wouldn't do to have her riding the trails all over the West. Gonna have to settle down a bit since we wanna have children."

Brock and Jimmy both turned and faced Huck. Brock responded, "You already thinking about having kids?"

"Not tomorrow, but pretty soon. I love Levi and miss Enyeto more than I ever thought I would. Sarah wants a big family, maybe even four kids. Says she missed not having any brothers or sisters growing up. Jimmy, she knows why and understands, but she wants to have lots a kids."

Before either of the fathers could respond, Kentaki held up his left hand, bringing all of the riders to a stop, saying as he did, "Walt said he saw five tracks?"

Gus answered, "He did."

"And I saw five that morning too. We got tracks here, Indians for sure, but only three."

Tom asked, "Whadda you think it means, Kentaki?"

"Direction they're coming from, not likely to be from the same five I saw. And I've got no idea if those are even the same five Walt saw. Means we've got at least eight riding around close, maybe more. I'm not seeing anything that makes me think they're hunters. The nearest tribe, friendly or not, is pretty far away."

Brock added, "Claude Pierre said the Sioux were getting riled up. Some coming back out this way from Dakota Territory. Said they didn't take to reservation life and want their land back. The land we're ranchin' on. Ridin' on. Kentaki, think that could be it?"

"Could be. Can't see anything else that makes any sense."

Brock, who had complete trust in Gus, asked, "Gus, whadda you think we should do?"

Gus looked around at the six other men and answered, "Long as we're out here, might as well trail 'em and see where it leads. Otherwise this is just a picnic. No offense, boys, but I prefer a pretty girl at my picnics."

BACK AT THE RANCH, the women were still seated around the table. Maria and Pukeheh had checked on Cisco, but it was clear he was healing well and would likely be up and about in the next week or so.

Sophie looked at Sarah and Maddie and said, "I'm so sorry."

Maddie asked, "About what?"

"When you dreamed of your wedding, I'll bet it didn't include having your new husbands riding off so soon, looking for, well, looking for Indians."

Before either woman could answer, Maria commented, "Now, Sophie, don't I remember that less than a week after your wedding, you and Brock hit the trails for New Mexico Territory? Looking for Brock's dad, I think. Man who abandoned him when he was only two years old. I'm guessing maybe not what you'd had in mind?"

Sophie nodded. "You're right. I can't even remember what I had in mind back then. Certainly can't remember my thoughts from before I met Brock. Thing is, through all of it, I wouldn't change a thing. Brock was meant to ride the trails and I was meant to be with Brock. I know if I asked him to settle down a bit he would. Maria, you remember, he even tried sheriffing in Dry Springs.

"I think he tried it for me, 'cept I never asked. About drove him crazy. No, even if I didn't really think enough about it, I knew what I was marrying. Doesn't mean there aren't hard days, hard times. But you can't have one without the other. Sarah, I'm sorry, but I think you married the same man. Brock and Huck may not be blood, but they couldn't be any more alike."

Sarah nodded. "Huck tried to tell me. I thought I understood, but what I really understood was that I was in love with Huck. And Sophie, you're right, my wedding dreams didn't include my new husband riding off to find Indians. Am I scared? Of course, I am. I'm only sixteen and I know that, but I've done more living in the last couple a months since we left Abilene than I did in all the years before. So yes, I'm a bit surprised about this morning. But if you ask me if I'd be anywhere else right now, with anyone else, besides Huck and all of you? Absolutely not."

13

FOREST

They followed the tracks for the rest of the day. Actually, six of them followed Kentaki, trusting that he was following the tracks. The conversation was sparse as all six spent most of their time scanning the area on all sides. The Sioux, if that's who they were following, were known to be fierce, pitiless warriors and the last thing they wanted was to be taken by surprise.

They rode through forests, rolling hills and open plains. The first time they left the forest for open plains, Jimmy asked, "Seems like we should maybe stay with these trees long as we can. I'd like to stay outta sight as long as possible."

Jimmy and Harry were the two in the group who'd never tangled with Indians in the wild, both having spent the better part of their adult years in the relative safety of Abilene. It was Gus who answered.

"You'd think so, Jimmy, but you'd be wrong. Thing about Indians is, and from what Claude Pierre tells me, especially about the Sioux, if they're looking for ya, they're gonna find you. No white man alive can hide from a determined Indian. What I'm saying is, if they're looking for us, they're gonna find us. Doesn't matter if it's in a forest, the plains, the top of a mountain or the bottom of a deep valley, they're gonna find us.

"Same time, if they don't wanna be found, that's not gonna be too easy either. Maybe a little better chance, 'cause we got Kentaki with us and from what I've seen, he's one of the best. So, best to stay in the open, give us a better chance of spottin' them before it's too late. Ain't guaranteed, 'cause an Indian can hide about anywhere, but it gives us a better chance."

Jimmy, looking a little paler than he had moments before, nodded and asked,

"If we can't find 'em anyway, what are we doing out here?"

This time it was Brock who answered. "Hate to say it, but we're using ourselves as bait. If they're friendly, we'll know soon enough and I'd like the CM to be as friendly with as many ranches and Indians as we can. Just makes life easier and since it's already hard enough, seems like a good idea. Now, if they're not friendly—and I fear that's the case—then I'd rather find out now. Better if we do what we need to do as far away from the ranch, from the women and children, as we can get.

"So, we'll keep following 'em until we know who they are and what they want. If it's trade, we'll have 'em ride back with us. If it's fightin' they want, we'll do that out here. Claude Pierre said the Sioux are riled up. Something about having moved to a reservation in Dakota Territory. Guess some of the young bucks didn't take to reservation life and came back to take what was theirs. We need to let them know right away the Circle CM is not where they want to try."

Harry looked at Jimmy and shook his head. "You never said nothing about being bait when we left Abilene."

Jimmy looked at his friend and smiled. "Didn't know. But Harry, would you really rather be back in Abilene, breaking up fights between drunk cowboys and arresting card sharks? I know I'd rather be here than back home frying eggs. Never felt so alive. Never felt so scared neither, but maybe that's part of it."

It was Huck who answered, "Harry, he's right, though this ain't for everyone."

Harry remarked, "I never said..."

Huck continued, "I know. Me and Tom and Kentaki, we talk about it all the time. I never knew anything but small town life until Brock rode into Dry Springs. Nothing wrong with it. My first dad, he was happy. If he'd never left Dry Springs, that woulda been okay with him."

Tom added, "Same for my folks. My dad's a lawyer in Dry Springs and I don't think he's even been to Denver in more than ten years." Looking at Jimmy and Harry, Tom kept going. "As I understand it, you both lived in Abilene for a long time. If Huck here hadn't come along and stolen your daughter's heart and then convinced her to move to way out here, you might both still be there, happy as can be.

"But maybe not. For me, Huck and Kentaki, once we saw what was out here, made it hard to think about ever going back. Kentaki, he even tried, went back to the canyon, but it didn't stick. It ain't that one's better than the other, least I don't think so. But a man's gotta figure out what's gonna make him happy, or maybe what's gonna drive him crazy."

Jimmy looked at Gus. "You're not sayin' much, Gus. Whadda you think 'bout all this?"

"Not sure I'm the right guy to look to for answers. Born and raised on a ranch and went to work on someone else's ranch when I was younger than these." He pointed at Huck and Tom and kept going. "Never knew anything else. Know I don't like cities or towns. Too many rules. Too many people. Not enough room. I get twitchy when I have to go to town.

"Lost a lotta good men. Lotta friends over the years.

This life can be... No, it is tough. Weather. Outlaws. Rustlers. Accidents. Indians. Surprises me a man could live as long as I have. But, by God, I feel alive every single day. Livin' by my wits and my guns. Figure I'll die on some trail someday. Maybe by myself. But I wouldn't trade it."

Jimmy turned his eyes toward Brock. "How 'bout you?"

"Left London a few years back. Biggest, greatest city in the world. Grew up there. Loved it. Came here looking for my father but found so much more. Haven't been back to London since I left. Miss my mom and my uncle, but I can't see ever going back. Like Gus said, this life, it gets under your skin, least it did mine, and then you can't live without it."

Harry laughed and said, "I just wanted to know why we were leaving the forest."

14

GRANT-KOHRS

They had set up camp the night before, well before dark, since no one was anxious to be riding in the dark not knowing if the tracks they were following were friend or foe. They broke the watch into three shifts with Kentaki and Huck taking the first, Jimmy and Harry the middle, and Brock and Gus, who were riding in now with the dawn, taking the last shift.

While Tom refused to acknowledge it, everyone could tell his shoulder was aching. Brock made sure he was the odd man out and could sleep through the night, which he did.

Huck and Jimmy got to work getting breakfast going. As Brock had explained the day before, if Indians were tracking them, they would already know they were there, so Huck wasn't too concerned about giving anything away with a fire. He and Jimmy heated up some beans, biscuits and antelope steaks along with a steaming hot pot of coffee —not too different from dinner the night before.

Jimmy took a bite of a biscuit covered with beans and commented, "Not sure how this would have done back at the restaurant, but food somehow tastes different out here. Better. Heard plenty of cowboys complain about trail food when they stepped into my place, but I'm not sure I get it."

Gus laughed as a he took a bite of antelope steak. "Food does taste better out here. Fresh air. The view. Feeling alive. Big appetites. A little part of you always wondering if it'll be your last meal. But don't get fooled, eat this same meal three times a day for a month while dragging behind a thousand head, trying to keep the dust outta your mouth, and some scrambled eggs an' orange juice brought to your table tastes pretty darn good."

Jimmy nodded as Kentaki rode back into camp. He'd left shortly before dawn to see what he could find. "Eight of 'em now, just like we thought. Those three we were following caught up to the five and they're all ridin' together. The three were moving easy, but the five were ridin' hard, coming from the west."

Gus asked, "Anything else?"

"Yep. Warriors for sure. No women. No children. No dogs. No pack horses. I don't know if they're Sioux, but I do know they're not friendly. Could be they're after another tribe, but warriors get worked up and kinda forget to be picky. They left moving fast once they got together, heading away from us. Might be they don't know we're here."

The men were quiet, thinking about what Kentaki had said, until Brock spoke.

"I think maybe we should ride over to Mr. Montgomery's place."

Jimmy asked, "Who's Mr. Montgomery?"

"William Montgomery. Owns the Grant-Kohrs ranch. Over ten million acres of prime ranchland. Bigger than the next dozen Montana ranches combined. Montgomery's a good man and his main ranch house is only about a half day's ride from here."

Jimmy asked another question. "What about the Indians we've been chasing? We just gonna give up?"

Brock looked around. "I've been thinking about that. We're two days from home and we haven't seen anything but tracks. Far as I can tell, they haven't done anything to anybody. Plus, they're heading away from us. Startin' to feel like we're looking for a fight and not just taking care of our own people. Figure we'd go talk to Mr. Montgomery. See if he's heard anything. Plus, I don't like all of us being gone from the ranch too long. Anyone got a better idea, I'm listening."

Huck wanted to say, *How 'bout heading home where my new wife is waiting for me*, but he knew he couldn't. Everyone agreed and after cleaning up, they changed direction and headed west toward the Grant-Kohrs ranch.

FOUR HOURS LATER, they rode past the large bunkhouses and stopped in front of the main house. Brock had been to the house a few times, but it was the first two visits that had been significant. The first time was to ask for Mr. Montgomery's help with Brock's growing feud with Clint Beck and the Boxed X. While Montgomery admitted he didn't like or trust Beck, he refused to help, other than committing to remain neutral.

The second time was for one of the Montana Cattlemen's Association meetings. They took place every other month and used to be held at Beck's Boxed X, but Montgomery had started to host them when Beck was going from bad to worse. A huge fight broke out between Beck and Brock and when Brock beat him, it seemed to push Beck over the edge, ending a couple of weeks later when Brock killed him in a gunfight.

Brock liked Montgomery and admired the ranch he'd built and the way he'd built it. Many of the things that he and Sophie were doing with the CM were based on ideas and suggestions from Montgomery, who had continued to host the Association meetings since Beck's death.

This time, as they rode in, Brock noticed a lot of activity. All of the men he saw were well armed. He dismounted from Horse just as Mr. Montgomery stepped out of the huge front doors.

"Afternoon, Brock, Huck. I'm afraid I don't know the rest of you, but you're welcome to set your horses up in the main barn and join me inside. Looks like you've been riding for a while and I can have some food and drink readied for you."

Brock and Huck handed their horses off to two of Montgomery's men while the others walked their own horses over to the barn.

As Brock and Huck started up the six wide steps leading to Montgomery's home, Huck said, "Thank you for asking us in. Looks like your men are a bit worked up. Mind if we ask what's happening?"

"Don't mind at all, Huck, and it's good to see you both. How about you give me a minute to get the food and drink started. That'll give your men time to join us and I'll tell you all at once. My guess is that is has to do with why you're here."

Brock and Huck looked at each other, then followed Montgomery into the house. Ten minutes later, all the men with the CM were seated and sipping hot coffee or tea with chipped ice. Brock introduced everyone to Montgomery and a couple of minutes later, Montgomery was joined by a man he introduced as Steve Merle.

"Steve's my foreman. Runs my ranch. Everything to do with men and cattle. I'm gonna let him tell you what's going on and then he has to leave."

Steve didn't hesitate and started right away. "Had a man

riding the line, Johnny Mac. Checking in with the men in the line shacks. Our men, two per, stay at the shacks for a week at a time, but we like to check in sometime during that week. Got more than a dozen shacks spread over the ranch. Johnny came in this morning, riding hard. Said he'd found two men dead, gunned down at a line shack almost a day's ride from here.

"From what he could tell, it was one hell of a battle, but in the end, my men were killed. Johnny looked around and found tracks for five horses. Came riding back hard, and now we're getting ready to go track down whoever did this."

Huck spoke next. "I'm sorry about your men, Steve, Mr. Montgomery. Let me guess on the tracks. Unshod?"

Johnny looked up at Huck. "They were. That why you're here?"

Huck answered, "It is. We haven't lost anyone yet, but we found tracks around the CM and we've been chasing 'em for two days. Thing is, now there's eight of 'em."

15

BREAKFAST

It was dawn on the second day since the men had left the ranch. Sarah, still in the habit of waking up early from all those mornings working at her father's restaurant, stepped into the kitchen. She was surprised to find Sophie already up, dressed and sipping a cup of coffee.

"Good morning, Sophie."

"Good morning, Sarah."

Sarah, still in her robe, poured herself a cup of coffee and added some sugar and milk. She picked up a biscuit from the previous night's supper and sat down. She took a bite of the biscuit and washed it down with a sip of coffee. The women sat in silence with Sarah watching the steam rise from her coffee mug and Sophie watching Sarah.

Sarah broke the silence, asking, "Do you normally wake up this early?"

"Not since Levi was little. We adopted Huck and Annabelle when they were older, so I don't know what all kids are like, but Levi was an early riser when he was a baby. But since he's been sleeping in more the last couple of years, so have I."

"But today?"

"I don't sleep much when Brock's gone."

"I'm used to the early mornings, but I'm not used to not sleeping at night."

Sophie asked, "You having trouble sleeping?"

"Just since Huck left."

Sophie stood up, walked over to the counter and helped herself to a biscuit. She added a little butter and some jam, then sat back down. She looked at Sarah and said, "Wish I could tell you it was going to get easier. But this is a hard life. So much of it is dangerous. Brock and Huck are different than most men. They seem to ride into danger, instead of away from it. When Brock rode into Dry Springs, and into my life, a little more than five years ago, I fell in love with him as soon as I met him.

"He'd walked into my father's general store and my father wound up inviting him to the house for supper. Brock walked up to the house while my father closed up the store and when he reached the bottom of the stairs, he looked up at me. I'd had men look at me before, but not like that.

"He tried to talk but he couldn't. Couldn't get a word to

come out. It was the cutest, most charming, most exciting thing I'd ever seen. Just when I thought he might turn away and never come back, my father walked up, introduced us and we started talking. Haven't stopped since. The thing is —and Brock doesn't know this—I couldn't have spoken then either. I'd never felt like that before, but I knew he was the man for me."

"How long...?"

"We got married very quickly. I was older than you when I met him. Dry Springs is a small town, but we got our share of visitors. Lots of men wanted to... wanted to talk to me, but none of them made my heart jump."

As Sophie took a sip of her coffee, Sarah spoke. "Abilene is a decent-sized town, I guess. Never really saw another one until we came here. We had plenty of cowboys coming through. They'd pay attention to me, least until Poppa came over with the meat cleaver. That always stopped them. Except Huck.

"I could tell right away he was different. Poppa could too, he just wasn't sure if he liked that or not. I know he wanted—wants—me to be happy. All he's ever wanted I guess. Did his best after my mother died, but he's not..."

Sophie filled in the blank. "He's not your mother."

"No. No, he's not. He did his best, still does, but I could never talk to him about..."

"Sarah, we haven't known each other very long at all. But you're married to my son and now we're family. It's easy to see why Huck fell for you. I understand why your father was concerned; mine was too. Good fathers want to protect their daughters. From pain. From trouble. And from men. They know that someday their little girl will fall in love and get married, it's just that they're never ready for it.

"After my mom died, it was hard. I used to talk to her about everything. After she died, my father tried, but there are certain things, things that are for a mother and her daughter. One day, Annabelle will come to me for those things. Brock? She goes to him for other things and that is good. But when she gets a little older... it'll be me. I guess I'm saying, if you want to talk, I'm here."

"Thank you, Sophie, and I do."

"You do?"

"I want to talk. I want to talk about Huck and I guess Brock and you and this morning."

Sophie sat quietly and let Sarah find her words.

"How do you do this?"

"Do?"

"How do you handle him being gone? Wondering if he'll come back and if he does... if he'll be hurt?"

Sophie took a bite of her biscuit, set it down and took Sarah's hand.

"I don't handle it well, honey. Right after we got married, we left for New Mexico Territory and started looking for his father. Seems like we've been on the trail pretty much ever since. We've been attacked by Indians and outlaws. Faced terrible weather. We've lost good friends. Brock has had to kill a lot of men. Huck and I have killed some. It's frightening every time, but I think I knew, at some level, the life I was going to have.

"Men like Brock, and your Huck, they have to live this life. If someone needs help, they're there. Every time. They're good at helping people, but they still get hurt. Thing is, there's no way to stop them or change them and, if I'm honest, I wouldn't want them to. Let me guess about something.

"I know this is new to you and I know in the short time you've been with my son, you've seen some terrible things, including him getting shot. But my guess is the last two nights have been the worst."

"They have. But I don't know why."

"It's because you're here and they're out there. The waiting? That's the worst part. I wish I could tell you different, but it never gets easier. At least when you're with them, no matter what's happening, you're with him."

Before Sarah could answer, Walt walked into the kitchen.

16

HISTORY

Mr. Montgomery looked at the seven men of the CM and at his own man, Steve Merle, and then spoke. "They are warriors and they are Sioux."

Everyone but Merle looked surprised at how confident Montgomery seemed to be as he made his statement. It was Brock who asked, "How do you know for sure?"

"I didn't. Until right now."

Huck asked, "Now? How do you know now?"

"Last week I was visited by a major in the United States Army. A man named Brian Sullivan. He came to see me. To warn me, really. Are any of you familiar with the Indian Peace Commission?"

They all shook their heads.

"I wasn't either. Happened back in '67. Your government

decided that moving Indians from this area to reservations would open up the land to settlers and traders. Make it safe for whites. The next year they met with the Sioux, as they had been meeting with all of the tribes in the territory. It took place at Fort Laramie. Laramie's about six hundred miles south of here, closer to the main Sioux home. But the Sioux did come up this far, hunting and raiding, so it made a difference to us.

"It's when I started my ranch. I was promised by the army that we would be safe. They moved the Sioux to the Black Hills, part of Dakota Territory. Called it the Great Sioux Reservation."

Tom asked, "So what happened?"

Montgomery answered, "The way Major Sullivan tells it, not all the Sioux thought it was so great. They are a warrior tribe, a warrior people. Their honor comes from battles, from counting coup, and the young ones can't do that on the reservation. So, about three months ago, eight of them left the reservation and headed west. As soon as you said there were eight, I knew. They've been killing and burning along the way from the reservation to here. Army's tried to capture them, but they haven't been successful.

"The major would deny saying this, but he believes the Sioux are the greatest horsemen on the plains. The army keeps trying the same thing, chasing them with a large group of soldiers. The major says the Sioux can hear them from a hundred miles away and they'll never catch them, but the army won't risk a small group of men, so Sullivan's hands are tied."

Huck, angry to discover that their neighbor had information on hostile Indians and kept it to himself, asks, "Mr. Montgomery, you said the major told you a week ago? Why didn't he tell the other ranches, or why didn't you?"

"Huck, that's a fair question, though you may not like the answer. The major thought the eight were heading this way. But he didn't know exactly where and he didn't think they'd get here this soon, if at all. We thought we had more time. We were wrong and I lost two men.

"As for the other ranches, I planned to tell everyone next week at the Cattlemen's Association meeting. Guess I shouldn't have waited, but the major seemed quite confident that we had at least that much time."

Brock, trying to make sure things stayed friendly, pushed forward. "Can't change any of that now. We should let the other ranches know. We certainly can't wait until next week."

Montgomery nodded. "You're right. I've got men leaving now to warn all the ranches in the Association. I assume you'll be riding back and I should tell my men not to stop at the CM?"

"Some of us will be riding back, so yes, consider us warned. Same for Katie and her ranch. She's staying with us and we'll tell her too."

Montgomery looked surprised. "Thank you, Brock, but you said some of you will be riding back? Not all of you?"

"No. We saw your men getting ready to ride. I'll send half our men back to the CM and the other half will ride with your men until we find the Sioux."

"Thank you, Brock, but that will not be necessary."

Huck, still angry that they hadn't been told and afraid of what might be happening at the CM ranch, blurted out, "Our men are as good as any in the territory."

Montgomery, fortunately, was a man slow to anger and recognized youthful passion. He looked at Huck and, with an understanding voice, addressed his comment. "Huck. Your men are most certainly the equal of any I've met, including any who ride for the GK ranch. I'd be proud to have you and any others who ride for the CM stand with my men. What I meant, and what I should have said, is that we have far more men than you do. I can better afford to have some of my men away from the ranch for what might be an extended search.

"I can do that and still take care of my cattle and the ranch. The CM is new and still growing, and as I understand it, you have recently added a few new people. It seems to me that you would all have an important role to play in defending your ranch and the people living there. As I said, I meant nothing negative by my comments, only that I believe your true value will be at the ranch."

Following a brief silence, Huck replied, "Mr. Montgomery, I'm sorry. I should have heard you out before react-ing. Please forgive me."

"Of course, Huck. I was your age once. While my wife had long since passed away, I was also married when I was a young man."

Huck, surprised, started to ask, "How did you—"

Montgomery laughed, breaking any remaining tension, and answered, "Huck, it's a big territory, but even still not much stays secret for very long—good or bad. This is obvi-ously good and I am happy for you. You too, Mr. Wheeler. I would never be so bold as to offer marital advice, but it would seem that the sooner you return to the CM, the happier everyone will be.

"Now, as part of my apology, please accept my invitation to supper and to stay until morning. We have plenty of food and plenty of lodging as well. My cook has been preparing the meal since you arrived. I believe if we move to the dining room, it should be waiting."

They walked into the elegant dining room, the site of the tremendous fistfight between Brock and Clint Beck a few months previously, and saw that Montgomery was correct and the table was set for ten.

The food was on silver platters in the middle of the table and each of the settings had China dishes and cloth napkins, along with crystal wine glasses. The platters were brimming with ham, chicken, steaks, vegetables and fruit as well as mashed potatoes. There was also milk, tea and wine. As they started to sit, Mr. Montgomery encouraged them to save room for dessert, as well as brandy and cigars.

Huck wasn't sure about anyone else, but he knew that he, Tom and Kentaki had never had such a formal meal. Brock had grown up in England and had some experience at the great tables of London. Huck was amazed at how at ease he looked.

As they took their seats, Brock asked Montgomery about his home country of Scotland, and he happily began telling tales of his homeland.

17

TOWN

When they had finished eating and had exhausted the conversation regarding the Sioux, Mr. Montgomery had dessert brought to the table. There were three of them and they were new to all of the guests, except Brock.

Montgomery explained as the men dug in that the first dessert was called cranachan. "It is what you would call a pudding. This one is made of whipped cream, toasted oats and raspberries. It is, as all three are this evening, a traditional Scottish dessert."

Brock was the first to comment. "I had these as a young man in London. I remember we had them with a variety of fruits, depending on what was in season."

Montgomery laughed. "It is the same here, though a true Scotsman will tell you that real cranachan must have raspberries. Our remoteness here can limit our choices, but we make do."

Huck, his anger—though not his concern—now forgotten, was enjoying a sample of the second dessert and managed, between bites, to ask what it was.

"That is Scottish shortbread. A rather simple recipe, but a favorite among many back home. Flour, butter and sugar are all that are needed and even here in the territory, those can easily be found. Huck, I'm happy to send you back with the recipe and would be honored if you and... I'm afraid..."

Since Huck's mouth was full, Gus answered for him. "Sarah. His wife's name is Sarah."

"Thank you, Gus. I would be honored if you and Sarah added the recipe to your family ones. It is a good thing for every family to have a little of Scotland in the kitchen. The last of the treats are Scottish scones. I will say it before Brock does, since he will undoubtedly tell you that Scottish scones can't measure up to the ones he grew up with in London.

"As silly as it sounds, I've seen otherwise good men come to blows over scones. I'd rather that didn't happen this evening, especially since I have seen Mr. Clemons in action when he is unhappy with someone." Montgomery pauses as everyone breaks out in laughter. "So I'll leave it to you to decide for yourselves. But I will say, if Mr. Clemons serves you his scones, you are always welcome here for the 'true' ones."

Brock good-naturedly responded, "I trust that this will never make its way back to my mother, but I have to admit, these are excellent."

The ten took their time working through the desserts and enjoying hot, strong coffee as they did. The conversation was light and enjoyable, as Brock and Montgomery shared stories of growing up in the United Kingdom and the differences between Scotland and England. Huck had never heard most of these stories and was fascinated to learn of Brock's upbringing. He wondered if he would ever travel to England.

The desserts finished, Montgomery invited everyone to join him in the sitting room. Brock and Huck accepted, but the others politely declined. The long, stressful couple of days and the large amount of food and wine had taken their toll. The promise of a comfortable bed and a long night's sleep proved to be too inviting to delay.

Montgomery arranged for sleeping quarters for the six men and then returned to the sitting room. Before taking his seat, he brought out a box of cigars, a bottle of brandy and three glasses. Brock and Huck accepted the offerings. The chairs they were offered were like nothing Huck had ever sat in before. They were huge chairs, made of incredibly comfortable leather. When he sat, he sank so deep, he wondered how easy it was going to be to get back out.

When the brandy was poured and the cigars lit, Montgomery spoke.

"Again, my apologies for not alerting you to the dangers we all face. While I am sure Major Sullivan would be shocked to find how quickly the Sioux had traveled, I should have been more cautious."

Brock waved him off. "You had no way of knowing. None of us did. I'm just sorry you lost two men. I am still uncomfortable not riding with you, but your position makes sense. I hope that you know that any time you or your men—"

"Mr. Clemons. Brock. We have not known each other long, but it does not take long to measure some men. I have no doubt that you will always do what is right and that you would never hesitate to help a friend or neighbor. Thank you for allowing me the same. Now, while I am sorry that the others are not joining us, I do have something I'd like to discuss with you."

Brock nodded. "Of course."

"As I understand things, the CM is planning to build a town on the trail between Bozeman and Missoula. Is that so?"

"It is. Sophie's father has taken over the planning for us. Years ago, he built a town in Colorado Territory. Dry Springs. It is where I met my Sophie—and Huck. He has found the land and begun planning. We were waiting for winter to end and plan to start soon. Probably as soon as this Sioux problem is cleared up."

Montgomery, nodding slowly, responded, "A town like this, it will be a lot of work."

"It will."

"And forgive my bluntness, it will also be quite expensive and require a tremendous amount of time to build?"

"Yes to both."

"I have been thinking about this town since I first heard of it. I believe it is an excellent idea. I am a little embarrassed that I did not think of it myself. Sending my men to Bozeman is costly in time and of course, dangerous. Having a town more than one hundred miles closer to my ranch will be a great benefit. It will benefit not only my ranch, but all of the ranches around here."

Huck sat up a bit in his chair and said, "My grandfather said it will also be good for travelers between Bozeman and Missoula and a good place for those who want to live close, but do not want to live on a ranch."

Montgomery nodded again. "You're right, Huck. A town like this will be good for all of us. And this is why I want to work with you and help build the town."

18

SEATTLE

It had been eighteen months since Finn and Anna Strauss had left New York. Anna had been hesitant to leave. Her family was in New York and it was all she had ever known. But her husband was a dreamer and he knew in his heart that their fortunes were to be found in Seattle, a growing city in the Territory of Washington. She also knew that it was her grandfather's dreams almost forty years ago that brought her family from Germany to New York.

Seattle was first settled by whites in 1851 and they even called the new town New York, which Finn thought was a good sign. The town's economy was based on timber and they supplied lumber to the much faster growing city of San Francisco to the south.

In 1867, the United States had acquired what is now

known as Alaska from Russia. The lure of gold was bringing many men through Seattle on their way north to chase their dreams, or on their way back south when they'd tried and failed. In December of 1869, it was officially incorporated as Seattle by the Territorial legislature. Railroads were being built.

Finn read about all of this in the *New York Times*. Having struggled for years without success to make a good living in the publishing industry, Seattle took a greater and greater hold on him. He finally convinced Anna to sell their small home, pack up their meager belongings and their two children, and move to Seattle.

Anna was reluctant, but she realized that Finn was not going to let this idea go. She agreed to try for a year, but he agreed that at the end of the year, if it wasn't working, they would move back to New York.

They took a sailing ship from New York to Panama. On this trip, Anna was horribly seasick and though she tried everything, she couldn't make it stop. Her two children, Noah, age nine, and Emilia, age six, loved the adventure at first. But after sailing to Panama, taking a train across the country and picking up another sailing ship that took them to Seattle by way of San Francisco, the children—and Anna —had had enough and simply wanted the trip to be over.

Six long months after leaving New York, they arrived in Seattle. Finn worked hard looking for a job or an opportunity that would make him wealthy and allow him to give his wife and children the life he knew they deserved. But the opportunities never materialized. The year passed quickly, at least for Finn. And when it had passed, Anna insisted they return to New York.

She also insisted, having sworn to never step foot on a boat again, that they return home by wagon, or at least until they could connect with a train that would bring them to the East Coast, her beloved New York and her family.

And this was how Anna found herself, and her family, a little over five hundred miles east of Seattle. They were almost a hundred miles south of Missoula, the last town they had seen and what she would consider as far from civilization—and New York—as she could possibly be.

She had no way of knowing that just south of where she and her family were there were two large ranches, the Circle CM and the Grant-Kohrs ranch. She also had no way of knowing that they would have been welcome guests at either ranch. So as nightfall came, they once again set up camp, the owls and coyotes the only sounds outside of their quiet conversations.

She started the fire while the kids gathered firewood and Finn took care of the horses and the wagon. She had no idea that she was being watched by eight Sioux warriors.

It didn't take the warriors long to realize that there were no more wagons coming. There was only one man and he didn't even know enough to carry his rifle with him everywhere he went. Their plan was simple and they doubted that there would be any trouble.

The eight mounted their ponies, unshod and with no saddles. They took only their rifles, leaving the rest of their belongings in the small camp. They were less than a half mile away when they started. They rode slowly and quietly at first, but as they drew closer, fearing nothing from the family, they started to gallop and let out their blood-curdling war cries.

None of the Strausses had time to react before the fury and power of the eight descended upon them. They were dead before they could even scream. Though they had no way of knowing it, it was merciful in a pitiful way. Many white travelers suffered horrible torture before finally being allowed to die.

Bodies were mutilated and four scalps were taken. Then the wagon was set on fire. Afterward, the eight Sioux warriors raced back to camp, screaming with the power of victory as they rode.

Two days later, drawn by the vultures circling overhead, the men from the GK ranch rode onto the scene. There were eight men, led by Nick Wale. They were tough men, hardened by the life they had chosen and the things they had seen and done. But none of the men were ready for the horrific sight in front of them. Two of them rode off quietly and threw up. Cowboys are a hard group of men, but none of the others so much as commented, knowing how close they were to following.

They drew their weapons and followed the tracks back to the Sioux camp, but the fire and the trail were cold. Nick insisted they bury what was left of the four victims and when they were done, they rode back to the Sioux camp and started trailing the Indians. Having lost two of their own men only three days previously, they were already motivated, but seeing a woman and her children slaughtered made the fires burn deeper.

It didn't take long for the men to figure out that the Sioux were heading straight for the Circle CM.

19

RETURN

The eight men returned to the CM late the following morning. They were well rested after their stay at the GK ranch. However, their concern had grown. While they had all held out hope that the Indians were friendly, it had been confirmed by the army and Mr. Montgomery that they were not.

Each of them understood that until the Sioux were hunted down and killed, none of them were safe. That also went for all other ranchers and homesteaders in the area. Having the support of the GK and the army was valuable, but Brock was used to handling things himself and grew increasingly uncomfortable with each passing mile as they made the ride back home.

Cole and a couple of the other men met them in front of the house. The three were armed and quite relieved to see that all eight men had returned and none had been injured or wounded. Their relief was short-lived as Gus explained what they'd learned from Mr. Montgomery. Huck, Tom, Brock and Jimmy were the first four off their horses, no doubt due to the fact they each had a woman they wanted to check on.

Huck was the fastest and was met by Sarah at the door. She leapt into his arms and whispered into his ear, "I missed you so much. Thank goodness you're safe."

He kissed her long and hard and whispered back, "I love you. It felt like three months, not three days."

As Sarah stepped back onto the porch. Jimmy and Brock were met by Maddie and Sophie, with hugs and kisses being shared. The big surprise was Claire. She came through the door, walked right up to Tom, wrapped her arms around his neck and kissed him square on the lips. No one was more surprised than Tom who was last kissed in public by his mother when he'd been about ten years old.

Claire then disentangled her arms, stepped back, placed her hands on her hips and with a pout on her face, said, "It's a good thing you came back, Tom James. I think I've decided I like you."

At that moment, Claire's sister, Katie, joined everyone on the crowded porch. Before Huck could respond, she said, "I certainly hope you have, little sister. I hate to think you go around kissing any man who you hadn't seen for a couple of days.

"Sophie, I really hope you don't mind, but I stepped into the kitchen and asked for some help in preparing a mid-day meal for a rather large group of people. I was hoping we could sit down together and learn what has been happening. While we're all grateful that everyone is back, safe and healthy, I would venture a guess that there are stories to tell and decisions to still to be made."

Sophie looked at Brock, who said, "She's right. About all of it. We are hungry, though we need to clean up first. There are stories to tell and there are some decisions to be made. It does make sense to do it all at once."

The women turned to head back into the house and the men turned the opposite way, getting ready to take care of their horses and then to clean up a little. As they did, they were all surprised when Jimmy started laughing. As they tried to figure out why, he spoke.

"Before I got married, I was worried about sharing my life with someone not named Sarah. I was used to making my own decisions and frankly, enjoyed my time alone. I really didn't know how I would feel about having someone, even someone I love, around all the time.

"I was also concerned about the slow pace of living out in the middle of nowhere. Things were always busy in Abilene, especially at the restaurant. Now, I haven't been here long and I just got married, but I think the last thing I have to worry about living here is being bored or having too much time with my wife. Now I'm worried about running myself to death on one hand and not getting to spend any time with my new bride on the other."

As his words sunk in, Sophie laughed and added, "Jimmy. Maddie. Actually all of you who are new here. Best you get used to it. There are quite a few words that can describe life on a large ranch, but at least for this one, boring is not one of them. As for time with Maddie, something tells me she'll make sure you'll find it. Now, let's all get going so we can sit down, eat and catch up on the last few days."

AN HOUR LATER, nearly twenty people gathered in the main house. Brock and Huck had spent most of that time with Annabelle and Levi, as much as they wanted to be with Sophie and Sarah. But as the two women watched their men play with the children, they both knew they'd picked the right man. The kids left when the conversation started, Annabelle now old enough to keep an eye on her brother for an hour or two.

The returning men were thrilled to see that Cisco was up and had joined them. He was moving slowly and was clearly in pain, but he was out of bed, seated and smiling.

Huck and Brock took turns bringing everyone up to

date on the GK ranch, Mr. Montgomery, the army and the Sioux. Everyone hated to hear about what had happened to the two GK ranch hands. Even the bravest among them feared the Sioux as a fierce and merciless enemy.

Brock explained how both the army and Mr. Montgomery had men out searching for the Sioux. He explained that he felt they still had a responsibility to join the hunt and it was never a good idea to just wait around for the enemy to attack. "Eventually, even the most committed will let their guard down and when they do..."

Just as Brock was wrapping up, there was a knock at the door. Since he was closest, Brock answered it. A man in an army unform stood on the porch, with a half dozen soldiers behind him, all still seated on their horses.

"Good afternoon. I am Major Brian Sullivan with the United States Army."

20

SULLIVAN

Major, welcome to our home. Your men are welcome to dismount and rest their horses in the livery."

"Thank you, but we won't be long. The others are outside the ranch, keeping watch, and these men will do the same from the inside. Are you Brock Clemons?"

By this time, Sophie had joined him at the door. Brock answered, "Yes. I'm Brock. This is my wife, Sophie. If you are in a hurry, perhaps we won't use up your time with what would obviously be a large number of introductions. However, allow me to introduce you to my son, Huck." Huck came forward and shook the major's hand. As he did Brock waved Kevin from his seat close to the kitchen up to the front door.

"And this is our dear friend Kevin, formerly known as

Major Kevin Calderwood of the United States Army. Not so long ago he was the commanding officer of Arizona's Fort Mojave, before leaving the military to follow us around the country."

Sullivan shook hands with Huck and Kevin, saying to Kevin as he did, "Major, it is a pleasure to meet you. I, along with most of us who serve out west, have heard about you and the work you did in Arizona. You have been missed."

"It's Kevin now. It's nice to hear that I have not been completely forgotten. I wish we had time to share some stories, but I heard you say that you are pressed for time?"

"I am." Sullivan looked at Brock and Kevin and asked, "Perhaps there is a quiet place where we can talk?"

Brock answered this time. "There is, Major, but it'd be best if Sophie and Huck joined us. Sophie runs the ranch, not me, and we keep no secrets from our son."

Brock excused the four from the others and asked Sullivan to follow him to Sophie's office, which he did. When they were all seated, Sullivan started. "I am sorry to have to tell you, but there are hostile Indians close. Eight of them according to our reports. We believe them to be Sioux and we believe them to be violent."

Brock stopped him and said, "Major, we have just come from the GK ranch, where you visited last week. I know you believed the Sioux were more than a couple of weeks away, but we now know that they're here..."

"How do you already know? We just found out this morning."

Huck, confused, added, "This morning? We found out yesterday when we stopped at the GK. Two of their men had been killed by Indians. Based on what we'd already thought and what you'd told Mr. Montgomery, we figured it was the Sioux. How did you find out this morning and still get here so quickly?"

Sullivan's chin dropped to his chest for a moment and then he lifted it, squared his shoulders and answered, "I did not know about Mr. Montgomery's men, though I am saddened to learn that they were killed. I wish I could say that I was surprised. We came across a terrible scene this morning, northeast and not too far from here.

"Four travelers in a wagon were slaughtered. Husband. Wife. Two kids. One of them a little girl. Tracks and a camp showed it was the eight Sioux. Not more than three hours from here. That's six people killed in three days. We have to assume they'll keep killing until they're stopped.

"Major... Kevin, you had a reputation as a man who could deal with hostile Indians. If you don't mind me asking, how did you do it?"

Kevin looked at Huck, Sophie and Brock, then answered. "You may not want to hear this, but I started by ignoring orders from those who'd never been out west. They had no idea how to find and destroy those who were killing our soldiers and civilians. Major, how many men do you have?"

"Twenty-five."

"Army orders to track the Sioux with no fewer than that?"

"Yes, that's accurate."

"Have you seen even a hint of the Sioux since you've been out?"

"Not a single time."

"And you've been out now almost two weeks?"

"That is also accurate."

"Major, you're never going to see them with that many men. You make too much noise, travel too slowly and leave tracks a child could follow. The Sioux know where you are at all times and probably know where you're going before you do. They don't attack because twenty-five well-armed men are too many, even for the skills that they have. But you'll never catch them."

Major Sullivan cocked his head and asked, "But didn't you have the same orders?"

"I did."

"And?"

"And I ignored them. Settlers, traders and my men were being picked off and it quickly became clear that by following orders, I was never going to stop them. I tried to get the orders changed but the officers above me were still using tactics they learned in the War Between the States

and those experiences were useless in pursuing and stop-
ping Indians. So I ignored them. Did I risk my career? I
guess so, but as long as I took care of the problem, I figured
no one was going to really care, even if they did find out."

"What would you have me do?"

"Major Sullivan. Brian. I can't tell you that. It is not my
command and it is not my career. What I can do is tell you
what I would do. After that, it's up to you."

"I'm listening."

"Do you have two good sergeants? Men you would trust
with other men's lives?"

"I do."

"Then I would split your command into three. Send
one group west back toward the GK. They have plenty of
men, but I don't know how many of them have ever had
more than a saloon fight. They need soldiers.

"I would send another north to Missoula. It's not likely
they'd attack the town, but there will be a lot of settlers
living in and around and they have no chance of protecting
themselves.

"The third group I would send east. This is the least
likely, but not impossible. If they do head east, maybe you
can surprise them."

"That makes a lot more sense than to keep chasing
ghosts and burying bodies. I'll order it now. Let's not forget,
they were not too far northeast of here a short while ago.
What do you plan to do about that?"

"I have a plan, but I need to run that by Brock first. He's my commanding officer now. He doesn't wear a uniform, but at least he listens to the men in the field. Good luck, Major, and I hope the next time we meet, we have enough time for cigars and bourbon."

21

LINE SHACK

As they stepped out of Sophie's office, they were met by Walt and Gus. Walt spoke first. "Sophie. Brock. I realize this is your ranch and we are your guests, but this impacts us and the Square M as much as it does you."

Before Brock could say a word, Gus added, "Same for me and my men. We ride for you and we ride for the brand, but on something like this... well, we oughtta be a part of it."

It was Sophie who answered. "You are both right and it was thoughtless of us. As far as that goes, Katie should have been with us too. However, at least for right now, action is more important than apologies."

Huck jumped in and explained to Walt and Gus, "The GK has sent men to chase the Sioux and the major is splitting his men into three separate companies and sending them north, west and east. Our own major, Kevin, is also about to share his plan with us."

Walt spoke again. "Before you do, Major Sullivan, I, along with Miss Katie and Miss Claire would like to accompany the men heading east. That's where our ranch is and we've been gone long enough. I was persuaded to stay until Brock and the others returned. Now that they have, it's time for us to leave."

Major Sullivan looked at Walt and asked, "Did you say the Square M?"

"I did."

"We were on our way there to warn you. How many in your party?"

"Myself, Miss Katie, who owns the ranch, and Miss Claire, her younger sister."

"Things have become too dangerous for you to make the trip alone. My troops will escort you to your front door and I will personally lead those troops."

Walking up behind the group, who were still standing in the hallway and Sophie's office, was Tom. He'd heard the last part of the conversation and without hesitation added, "If Miss Claire is riding back, I'll be riding with her."

Huck looked at his friend and asked, "Does she know? How will you get back? Tom, it's too dangerous to return by yourself."

"I'll be staying at the Square M until this passes."

This time it was Sophie with a question. "Does Miss Katie or Miss Claire know about your plan?"

"They do not. I will let them know now. Major, how long before we leave?"

"Fifteen minutes."

"We'll be ready." Tom turned around and headed back to the main room to find Katie and Claire. Walt followed.

Major Sullivan looked at Brock and Sophie, saying, "I believe it is time for me to get my men ready for the new approach. Kevin, thank you. Your insight has been invaluable. I am certain that we will see each other again, hopefully sooner than later. I look forward to it already."

Kevin smiled at Sullivan and said, "Don't thank me until you know if it worked and how those back east take to the news when they find out. But I look forward to that drink and cigar regardless."

Sullivan said his goodbyes and left in a hurry. Kevin looked at those remaining and said, "Let's step back inside Sophie's office for a minute. I have a plan, but we're going to need to move quickly. Gus, best you be here too."

Four hours later, Sergeant Lanny Harris and his seven men were more than halfway back to the GK ranch. Sergeant Thurman Buckner was still heading north with his eight men and Major Brian Sullivan and his seven men were dismounting in front of the main house of the Square M. Walt, Tom, Miss Katie and Miss Claire were with them. Katie insisted that the men spend the night at the ranch, split between the main house and the bunkhouse. She also insisted that they all share a meal together.

Meanwhile, the men of the CM were only a mile from their northernmost line shack. The CM had three line shacks in place, with plans for at least three more. Larger ranches used them to house the men who were working the far reaches of their ranches. It was a much better use of their time than having them ride back and forth, was far more comfortable than throwing down their bedroll, and most important, the thick wood walls offered protection against the elements and hopefully, against any attackers.

Frankie Russo and Deke Hankins were the two men working the northern part of the ranch and had been staying at the line shack for five days. They were surprised when Huck rode up. While Huck worked hard, he didn't work the cattle or stay in the line shacks. As far as Frankie and Deke knew, he'd never been to one before.

Frankie welcomed Huck and suggested he tie off his horse and come inside for coffee and a bite to eat. He knew he'd explain why he was there when he was ready.

Huck did as he was asked and as soon as he had the hot coffee in his hand, he told them about the Sioux, the killing of the GK ranch hands and the slaughter of the travelers.

Since they'd been away for five nights, they'd heard none of it. Both men were surprised and concerned.

The surprise and concern grew as Huck continued, "The wagon train, where the family was murdered, was less than three hours from here. Plus, we know they're willing to attack line shacks. Means there's a pretty good chance this is the next place they'll hit."

Deke, who was warming up some mountain lion steaks and beans, turned to look at Huck. "Don't mean anything by this, Huck—we both know you got sand—but if there's eight of 'em, what do you think the three of us are gonna do? Woulda thought maybe you'd bring some more men."

"That's fair—and we did. Gus, Brock, Kentaki, Kevin, Ten and Willy were with me. Well, not with me, but they're close."

Deke, sounding even more concerned, asked, "Whadda you mean 'were' with you? Where are they now? What happened?"

22

THE PLAN

Huck answered, "They're safe."

Deke, along with Frankie, remained confused. "If they came with you and they're safe, where are they?"

Frankie added, "If we got eight crazy Indians headed our way, seems like we could use every man."

Huck said, "We can and we are. Let me explain. About a mile back, we split up. Gus, Brock and Kentaki are hunkered down a little west of us, and Kevin, Ten and Willy are doing the same, only a bit east of us. And I'm here.

"Now before you say anything, I know I told you that the Sioux are north of us, least they were last we knew. Reason we don't ride north after them is, much as I hate to say it, we wouldn't be able to find 'em. Maybe one or two of us could, 'specially if Kentaki was one of 'em. We might be able to find them and maybe even sneak up on 'em. But there's no two of us could defeat eight Sioux warriors.

"But the ten of us can. Thing about that is the ten of us can't get ourselves close enough to fight 'em. Army's been chasing 'em for weeks and haven't seen them once. So, since we can't track 'em down with enough men to go to battle, we thought we'd bring 'em to us. Kevin's idea actually."

Frankie was the first of the two to get it. "You mean you're using me and Deke as bait? We're supposed to wait here until eight Sioux warriors come racing down on top of us?"

"That's not exactly how Kevin put it, but yeah, I guess that's about it. 'Course it's not just you and Deke. I'm here too."

Deke, not comforted by that, said, "Huck, you're a good man in a fight. Seen you with fists and guns and you're as tough as any of us, but how we gonna hold off eight Sioux?"

"That's where Kevin's plan comes in. We only need to hold them off for about five minutes. They'll hear the first shots fired and the six of them will come racing in from two sides and up the middle. Guns blazing. The Sioux will never expect it and won't be ready for it. All we gotta do is stay alive and keep 'em busy for five minutes."

Deke, still not thrilled, continued, "And what if they

pick us off outside before the others get a chance to get here?"

"Kevin thought of that too. Starting now, we don't leave the cabin. Not for any reason. Sioux will see the three horses in the corral. That won't spook 'em. We'll keep a fire going. Smoke'll let 'em know we're here. Keep the windows closed, the door barred and weapons ready."

Frankie asked this time, "And we just sit here, inside this box and wait until we're attacked?"

"Yep. We can eat supper and play a little cards if you like. Comes time to bed down, one of us stays awake at all times and the other two can sleep. If they don't come tonight, we stay here tomorrow and do the same thing."

Deke shook his head. "Damndest thing I ever heard of. We're gonna sit here and play cards and wait for Sioux Indians to come find us."

Huck looked at both men. "Well, I am. We can't find 'em and we can't wait around while they keep picking off men. And women. And children. You don't want to do this, I understand. Not thrilled about it myself. You're welcome to saddle up and head back to the bunk house. Wouldn't think less of ya if you did."

Deke said, "Ah, hell, Huck. Didn't say we wouldn't do it. 'Course we'll do it. Don't really matter if you'd think less of us. We would. And anyway, didn't say we wouldn't do it. Just said it's the damnnest thing I ever heard of. And it is."

Sᴇʀɢᴇᴀɴᴛ Lᴀɴɴʏ Hᴀʀʀɪs and his seven men rode up to the main house of the GK ranch. It was late, well after dark, but they were still greeted by a half dozen well-armed men.

Moments later, Mr. Montgomery opened the front doors and stepped out onto the huge porch. He was quite concerned when he saw only eight men. He knew there had been twenty-five when they first visited. He looked over at his men and said, "Thank you, gentlemen. As you can see, these are not the Sioux. While I learn what has happened, please continue your watch. Sergeant, I hope that the rest of Major Sullivan's men are safe, but please dismount and explain."

Sergeant Harris did as he was asked and his men did the same. "Mr. Montgomery?"

"Yes."

"We did not meet when we first visited your ranch. I was with the men who waited while Major Sullivan visited. As for the other men, including Major Sullivan, they are all well. At least they were earlier today when we left them."

Montgomery nodded. "Would you like to come inside and explain what is happening? If you plan to stay until morning, your men are welcome to put their horses in the livery and find beds in the bunk house. There is always stew and coffee ready and they should help themselves to whatever they would like."

"Thank you, sir." Harris turned back to his men. "Let's do as Mr. Montgomery suggested." He turned back and remarked, "My men are ready to stand watch with yours."

"That won't be necessary, Sergeant. I'm guessing you and your men have ridden hard today and would welcome the sleep. I have plenty of men to stand guard."

The men had ridden hard and did welcome the break, the coffee and the food. They did what Mr. Montgomery suggested and what Sergeant Harris allowed.

Harris followed Montgomery into the house and the two sat down, Harris accepting a small glass of brandy— which he had never had before. He took a sip and then started to explain how things had changed since the last time they had visited.

23

WAITING

At about the same time that Sergeant Harris and Mr. Montgomery were enjoying a glass of brandy, Deke sat alone at the small table inside the line shack listening for Sioux Indians while Huck and Frankie slept. And what would have seemed like a world away to Deke, Tom sat on the front porch of the Square M main house, sipping a cup of coffee and the savoring the company of Miss Claire.

While he was listening to her talk (and enjoying every minute), he was also letting his mind wander a bit and wondered if life could really be this good. Was it possible that he could spend all of his nights listening to Miss Claire? He knew it was crazy to think she could fall for someone like him, but she did kiss him in front of everyone and she was sitting on the porch with him right now.

"...coming here was supposed to be an adventure, but I was always going to go back to St. Louis. Walt brought me along so that I could see my sister while they took care of matters that needed taking care of after our father died. This was going to be the year of my 'coming out' party."

Tom had no idea what a 'coming out' party was and at first was embarrassed by that, but then decided it was best to ask. There were going to be plenty of things Claire knew about that he didn't, and he might as well get used to it. He never thought about all of the things he knew that she didn't, but even if he had, he wouldn't have realized how important they were.

"I'm sorry, but I have no idea what a 'coming out' party is. Coming out from what?"

Claire laughed, a sound that always filled Tom's heart, and answered, "In proper society, a young woman is 'introduced' formally. In a way, it's a bit odd, since she is being introduced to people she has known her whole life. But it's a tradition and a fun one. There are many guests, musicians, excellent food and the young women—me—get to dress up in beautiful gowns. If you were there, you would be wearing tails."

"Tails?"

Claire laughed again. "It is part of formal attire for young gentlemen. You would have a top hat, a black suit with a white tie, and the suit coat would be quite long, the 'tails.' You would be very handsome, of course, and might even ask me for a dance."

"I don't know how to dance. I have never been to one."

"Well, then, Mr. Thomas James, I shall have to teach you. That way, when we visit St. Louis, you will be prepared."

All Tom heard was 'when we visit St. Louis.' His mind raced as he tried to grasp what that meant. He also tried to imagine what Claire would look like in a formal gown. He also wondered where he would ever find a top hat and tails and how he would pay for them if he did. Claire, with a lilt in her voice, kept talking and Tom was sure of one thing— he had never been so happy in his entire life.

WHILE TOM SAT on a front porch with the girl of his dreams, Gus, Kentaki and Brock were sitting in the cold, with no fire, no coffee and no conversation. While Gus was the one on watch, neither Brock nor Kentaki could sleep. They imagined the same was happening with Kevin, Ten and Willy across the way.

While the six men knew that the Sioux were normally reluctant to attack at night, none of them were willing to count on that to the point of relaxing. And while Brock and Kentaki trusted Gus to keep watch, it didn't mean that they were able to sleep.

It was the same across the way where Kevin was responsible for making sure nothing happened. Ten and Willy were both wide awake. All six men had a feeling that something was going to happen in the morning. They could use the sleep, along with a hot meal and a cup of steaming coffee, but none of those things were going to happen.

Willy, to the endless irritation of his long-time partner Ten, had trouble being awake and not talking, whispered, "Craziest thing we've ever done. Sitting around hoping to get attacked by the Sioux."

Ten, who often simply didn't respond to Willy, something that rarely impacted his friend enough for him to stop talking, answered this time.

"I said let's keep doing stagecoaches. We were good at it and we knew what to do. Let's retire, you said. It'll be good to sit around for a while and relax. And now, we're sitting somewhere in the freezing cold, hoping to be attacked by Sioux and then—if we survive—we're gonna build a saloon in a town that doesn't exist in the coldest place we've ever been. Not sure exactly what you meant by relaxing, but this sure as hell ain't it. By God, Willy, if the Sioux don't kill ya, I just might."

In the more than ten years they'd ridden together, that was most words Willy had ever heard Ten speak at one time. It was all he could do to not laugh at his friend.

Before Willy could answer, he heard Kevin whisper,

"You girls best save your dickering until after we've dealt with the Sioux. For now, keep quiet so I can listen."

They did, but Willy knew he had plenty to say come morning. Ten knew it too; he just wasn't as happy about it as Willy was.

Gus, Brock and Kentaki remained quiet, each lost in their own thoughts and each straining to hear the smallest sound that might indicate the Sioux were near. Like most men, they found the waiting the hardest part, harder even than the actual battle. All three were men of action and not used to waiting. Even Kentaki, who had the most patience of any of them, was struggling with the impulse to get up and do something, anything, instead of just lying there.

Morning was still six hours away.

24

EMILY

It was an hour before dawn. It was dark and cold, which has a way of preying on a man's mind. Sergeant Lanny Harris and his seven men slept well inside the protection of the GK ranch. The GK ranch hands, who'd left three days earlier, hadn't found a single track and had decided to ride back to the ranch after a hot breakfast. The eight men who'd ridden north under the command of Sergeant Thurman Buckner were just starting their morning, after an uneventful night.

At the Square M, Major Brian Sullivan was enjoying a moment alone in the kitchen, having started the fire and heated the coffee. He knew his men would be stirring in the bunkhouse and he was trying to decide where to go next. It ate away at him that he hadn't found the Sioux, especially now that people were dying, people he had sworn to protect.

Tom and Claire sat awake in their separate beds, in separate rooms, both wrestling with the same questions, the same emotions. Each was wondering about their future, hoping it included the other.

Inside the line shack, all three men were awake. They felt bad for their friends outside who they knew had to be cold, with no prospect of a hot breakfast or a cup of coffee. Of course, while they could still have a fire inside, and according to the plan should have, they were still bait sitting in a trap, an uncomfortable feeling for any man.

They had pistols and rifles sitting underneath both windows and by the only door. They had checked and rechecked the weapons to make sure they were clean, loaded and ready for battle. Ammunition had been laid out on small tables at each of the three spots. The men knew there was nothing to do but wait.

They trusted the men outside, quite literally with their lives, since all three knew they could not survive an attack alone against eight Sioux warriors. But they were committed now, so waiting—and praying—were their only options.

Frankie, who enjoyed cooking, started to get breakfast going. His family had been in the restaurant business in New York, and Frankie had started working there when he was very young. His family were recent immigrants to the

United States, having come over from Italy, and they didn't have enough money to prioritize education over work. For the family to survive, to make try and make their mark in New York City, everyone had to work.

The work was hard, but he loved his family, especially his uncle. While Italian women were world-renowned for their recipes and their cooking, Uncle Lorenzo was the best cook in the family. He took great joy in sharing his secrets with Little Frankie and Frankie loved learning. His cooking was what made Frankie the most popular bunk mate when work duties were split up at the ranch.

When the coffee was boiling, Frankie added his two special ingredients—a little bit of chocolate and a dash of cinnamon. He carried both with him everywhere he went. Everyone knew when they went into Bozeman to pick up supplies, to always pick up chocolate and cinnamon for Frankie. They never made him pay.

The coffee done, he poured a mug for Huck and another for Deke and handed it to them. He then turned his attention to food. This morning would be biscuits, huge and browned to perfection, and then gravy. Frankie's gravy was always thick, with plenty of meat. Back in New York, his uncle would add cornstarch to his gravy, which thickened it up. But cornstarch was hard to come by in Montana Territory, so Frankie made do with flour, which was easier to get and was a staple on the shelves of every line shack.

When it was ready, he served up three plates, handing

one each to Huck and Deke and setting the third one down in front of his seat. He poured himself a cup of coffee and joined them at the table.

Having talked about the Sioux enough for all of them, Huck turned to Deke and asked, "Deke, do I remember you have a daughter?"

Deke, a huge smile spreading across his face, said, "I do. Emily. She'll be seven now. Prettiest little girl you ever did see. Her momma's pretty too. Always was. We grew up together, but not really, you know?"

Huck looked at Frankie and seeing he didn't know either, said, "No, I don't know. Sorry."

"Her momma, Sadie, was always a looker. Her family had money and mine didn't. In Dayton, Ohio that means a lot, least it did to her old man. He was a banker and Sadie was his only child. We met and fell in love, the way kids do.

"Her father hated the idea and tried everything to keep us apart. Even sent a couple guys to rough me up one time. I whooped 'em both. Funny part was, the more he tried to keep us apart, the more we struggled to be together. Even I knew enough to know that's the way it was with kids and parents. Well, the way things happen sometimes, one day we woke up and Sadie was with child.

"A few nights later, after the restaurant closed, I stepped out the back door to lock up and there he stood, with three tough guys with him. I figured I was in for it, but he said he just wanted to talk. The three guys were there to make sure

I listened. He told me he'd found out about Sadie and knew it was mine. Told me he'd never let me be around Sadie or the baby. Never. Would do anything it took to make sure.

"I looked at him and looked at the three thugs he'd brought with him and I knew he was telling the truth. I wouldn't even be able to get into the house and take her away. Not that I had anywhere to go, or any money to take care of her and the baby if we did.

"He said he was giving me a thousand dollars to get out of town and never bother his family again. Offered me an envelope. When I didn't take it, he dropped it on the ground and said, 'Take it or don't, but I better not see you anywhere near my family.' Then he turned and walked away.

"I knew he meant it and that I couldn't fight him. Not with his money and those men. I picked up the envelope and walked back inside the restaurant. Sat up most of the night trying to figure out what to do. Finally decided I had to leave. It would be too hard to stay in town and not see Sadie and the baby and even if I tried, it would be miserable for her.

"I fell asleep inside the restaurant and when I woke up, my uncle and my parents were there, getting ready for the breakfast crowd. I explained everything. My mom cried, of course, but they all understood. I gave them the envelope and headed west. Seven years later, here I am.

"Sadie, she gets notes to my mom and mom mails 'em to me. Her father doesn't know. She's moved on and is married to someone her father approves of, so it's real nice she does that. The notes come about twice a year. This year, I got notes from Emily too."

Frankie was about to say something when the first shot shattered the moment and the silence.

25

BATTLE

The Sioux were young and inexperienced. They were also fearless, excellent shots and matchless riders, and they focused all their attention on the men inside the line shack.

The first shot was followed by plenty more, the warriors making no effort to hide their presence, confident that surprise and their numerical advantage would win the day. The shack backed up to a hill. Both sides were windowless and doorless, so they focused their efforts on the front side, as Kevin knew they would.

Huck, Deke and Frankie had leapt from the table to the windows and the door, the pent up energy and nervousness relishing the relief. The door and both windows had gun slits in them and the three men slid them open and opened fire. The advantage of the gun slits was that it was very unlikely that a bullet would make its way through them. At the same time, the field of vision was limited, which made hitting someone difficult.

That didn't stop the men from shooting. They knew they had to engage the Sioux and keep their focus on the cabin. They knew that eventually, the Sioux would grow frustrated and likely set fire to the cabin, which was the real danger for the men inside. This morning, that was not going to be an issue.

Over a minute had passed since the first shot and in that time, the six men who'd been waiting had saddled up and had started the mile ride. As determined the day before, Kentaki and Gus would be riding up on the cabin's righthand side, Ten and Willy on the left, and Kevin and Brock would be riding straight up the middle.

It was hoped this would leave no way out for Sioux, but none of the men underestimated their riding—or shooting—ability. Huck knew the Sioux wouldn't be able to hear the riders any better than he could. With luck, the riders would be close before the warriors had any idea. One of the Sioux, he looked to Huck to be younger than he was, decided to show his courage by charging the cabin.

Huck was surprised but knew this was his chance. He leveled his Winchester 1873 and took aim. When the warrior was only twenty feet away, Huck fired two quick shots. The man dropped to the dirt and his horse took off at a gallop. Deke saw what happened and wanting no surprises later, put two more bullets into the fallen man, ensuring he was dead.

This enraged the Sioux and they redoubled their efforts, pouring shots at the cabin as fast as they could fire and reload. Huck, looking carefully from a corner of the slit, saw two horses racing up from directly in front of him. He knew that would be Kevin and Brock.

They were firing as they approached, both with pistols since they had anticipated close-quarter shooting. The Sioux looked surprised, but to their credit, the seven remaining warriors whirled as if they were one and turned to face the two men who seemed to be firing nonstop.

Just as the warriors brought up their rifles, Gus and Kentaki from one side and Ten and Willy from the other joined the battle. Even with all the pistols and rifles going off, Ten's ten-gauge roared above the rest. Huck, Deke and Frankie kept on firing. After a minute or so, they threw open the door and windows to give them better shots.

The Sioux were outnumbered, but their horses were smaller and quicker and they seemed to move without any effort from the Sioux. Huck watched in horror as Willy was hit and thrown from his horse. One of the Sioux rode over, hatchet in his hand, ready to finish off the wounded man. Huck stepped out onto the porch, lifted his 1873 and dropped the Indian from his horse. Ten, who'd seen his friend fall, put two rounds from his ten-gauge into the fallen Sioux and now two of them were dead.

Huck heard a scream from inside the shack and knew that Deke or Frankie had been hit. He trusted that whoever hadn't been hit would look after whoever had been and he kept shooting.

The danger for all the combatants increased as they all drew together. It seemed to Huck that the men were just as likely to hit one of their own as they were one of their enemy.

Without any warning, one of the Indians broke and headed west. Without a word being spoken, Kentaki and Ten took off after him. In their travels, Huck had seen both men chase Indians and outlaws and knew that the one who had run would be dead very soon. His horse was quick and he was a better rider, even better than Kentaki, but Kentaki and Ten had horses built for endurance. They would not give up and they would catch Indian.

With Willy, Deke and Frankie out of the fight and Ten and Kentaki gone, that left Gus, Brock, Kevin and Huck to battle the remaining five Sioux. Two of the Sioux suddenly seemed to remember Huck and the fact that he wasn't on horseback. With a signal that Huck couldn't see, they both wheeled toward him and charged the shack, guns blazing.

Brock saw them at almost that instant and turned Horse to join the fray. He had a Remington 1858 in one hand and the reins in the other. Firing non-stop, he hit one of the two. The Indian slid from his horse, dead before he hit the ground. The second one, sense having been replaced by passion, leapt from his horse and landed on Huck, knocking him back against the shack.

Huck shook his head, more surprised than hurt, dropped his empty pistol and struck out with his right hand, smashing it into the temple of the warrior. They were about the same age and size, and the warrior was certainly game.

The Indian shook off the punch and landed one of his own in Huck's gut, knocking out most of his wind. Knowing his life hung in the balance, Huck hugged the Indian and drew him close and tight, hoping to use the moment to catch his breath.

He never saw the other Sioux coming.

26

GUS

Gus saw the Indian coming down on Huck and raced toward the shack. He, like most, was out of ammunition. As fast as the horses were moving, there was no way to reload. When he got close, he jumped off his horse and tackled the warrior just before he reached Huck and the Indian he was already fighting.

The Indian was young and strong. Even though Gus was his senior by more than thirty years, he was still tough and seasoned. He'd been in plenty of barfights in his life, though he knew this one wasn't going to end with a bloody nose or a broken jaw, but would only end when one of them was dead.

He wrestled the man to the ground, which kept him from attacking Huck, but the Sioux had obviously been in a few fights himself. He tried to knee Gus in the groin, but

Gus was ready for that and stopped him. Gus landed two good shots in the man's ribs and thought he felt them break with the second punch. To the Indian's credit, he never stopped fighting and tried to gouge Gus' eyes out. He managed to bloody one before Gus could pull his hands away, but he'd blinded Gus in one eye, at least for the duration of the fight.

Each side had two men left on horseback. Kevin and Brock had to focus their attention on the two mounted Sioux and could only pray that Gus and Huck could handle the men they were fighting.

Huck had sucked in enough oxygen so that he could keep fighting. He dropped both hands and started driving them into the warrior's gut and ribs. He felt the ribs give and heard the Indian gasp in pain as Huck drove punch after punch into his gut. The man was weakening, but in no way was he giving up. Huck knew if it was a barfight, it would be over. They two would be pulled apart and each would live to fight another day.

But not today. Not this fight. The man facing Huck had no quit in him and there was no one to pull them apart and yell 'enough.' This wasn't going to end until one of them was dead. Somehow the warrior gathered enough strength to ignore the pain and the broken ribs and land a punch in Huck's face that knocked him back into the shack. Ignoring the pain and without hesitation, he charged forward and slammed into Huck.

Ten feet away, Gus and the warrior were still on the ground. Experience and toughness was holding its own against youth and strength, but if anyone had been able to watch, they would have seen that Gus was fading, drawing on the last of his resources and the last of his strength.

Five minutes and three miles after they'd started after the lone warrior, Kentaki and Ten caught him. Kentaki raised his hatchet, ready to sweep the man from his horse, but before he could, Ten blasted him off his horse with his ten-gauge. A second shot made sure he was dead. Without a word, the two turned and raced back to the line shack, ready to help their friends.

Inside, Deke was bleeding badly. He'd been shot in the face and Frankie didn't think he had much time left. He wanted to get back into the fight, but he just couldn't pull himself away from his dying friend. They'd ridden too many miles together, been through too much together for him to let him die alone.

Deke couldn't move his mouth because of the gunshot wound, but Frankie could see in his eyes that he knew he was dying. Tears poured down Frankie's face as much from frustration about not being able to help as from the pain of knowing his friend was leaving him.

He was too good of a friend to lie to Deke, so instead he said, "Deke, it doesn't look good." Deke blinked. "I know where you keep your letters and I'll write one to your folks and to Emily. I'll tell her what a brave man you were and how much you loved her. Deke, I ain't ever gonna find someone like you to ride the trails with. You were a good man."

Frankie had closed his eyes to try and blink away the tears and when he opened them, his friend was dead. He grabbed the cushion from the chair next to the window and gently moved his friend's head from his lap to the cushion. He said a very quick prayer, grabbed his pistol and headed out the door to the porch.

As he did, he saw Huck push back against the Indian he was fighting. Before Frankie could get off a shot, Huck hit him with a tremendous right hand. The warrior's head snapped back and he toppled over, crashing down the porch stairs. Huck and Frankie could see that the man's neck was broken. They didn't know if it was from the punch or the fall, but it didn't matter. He was dead.

One of the two mounted Indians made the mistake of turning in front of both Brock and Kevin. Both men had somehow found a way to reload in the midst of all this and neither missed as they fired at the man directly in front of them.

The last of the mounted Sioux turned back to face Brock, Kevin, Huck and Frankie. Huck saw that he was headed for Brock, but his gun was empty and on the floor. As he reached for his knife, anything to stay in the battle, four quick shots went off next to him. He saw the Indian drop and turned to see Frankie's gun smoking.

That left one Indian—the one fighting Gus. The men had both gotten to their feet and were grappling. Kevin rode close and seeing Gus was in trouble risked shooting into the fight. Both shots were true and the Indian died on the porch, a long knife slipping from his hand as he fell.

27

FINAL SPOTS

It was as if the surviving men all took one, long, deep, collective breath. As they did, Kentaki and Ten came racing back and pulled up in front of the shack. They all knew that meant the Sioux they had chased was dead. The entire battle lasted less than fifteen minutes, but the results would last a lot longer.

When Ten saw that it was over, he jumped off his horse and ran to Willy. This set everyone back into motion. Gus, his back to the shack wall, slid slowly to the porch. Brock and Huck were there almost before he stopped.

Frankie turned slowly and walked back into the shack. Kentaki, sensing that something was wrong, dismounted and followed him. Kevin went to each Indian and made sure they were all dead, which they were. Seven bodies were scattered around the dirt.

Ten leaned over his friend. "Where you hit?"

"My side."

"Is it bad?"

"Of course, it's bad. It's a gunshot. Not as bad as that time down in the Panhandle. Remember that? Those bandits came outta nowhere. You got two right away with that shotgun a yours..."

Ten shook his head. "Even when you're shot, you still can't shut up. Least stay quiet till I get you patched up. Then maybe you can get one a these others to listen to you for a while."

Willy started to laugh, but it hurt too much. Not so much that he couldn't keep talking though. "Admit it, Ten, you'd miss me if I was gone. You'd sit out on the porch and ask the gods to bring me back, just to tell you one more story."

"Willy, if the gods listened to me, you'da shut up a long time ago."

"Anyway, you got two of 'em right away, but there was two more..."

Ten did what he always did when Willy was telling the same story for what felt like the fiftieth time, he tuned him out and focused on what needed to be done. And what needed to be done now was to get Willy into the shack, get him cleaned up, and see if that bullet went clean through or had to be taken out.

Inside the shack, Kevin found Kentaki and Frankie

kneeling next to Deke. It didn't take much to tell that Deke had been killed, or how strongly Frankie felt about his friend. Kevin, as gently as he could, spoke to Frankie. "Frankie, I'm real sorry about Deke. I didn't know him long, but he was a good man, and from what I can tell, a good friend. Just bad luck. Damned bad luck. You want we should bury him here, or we can take him back to the ranch and bury him there. We'll do whatever you want."

Frankie looked up, no longer trying to hide his tears, and answered, "No, he died here, he should be buried here. That way he can watch over me when I'm here, just like he did when he was alive. I'd like to sit with him for a little bit longer, if that's okay."

It was Kentaki, standing up, who answered. "You take all the time you need. You got a special place up here where you think he'd like to be buried?"

Frankie thought for a moment and then answered, "I do. I mean, there is. When you step outside, there's a little trail off to the right. Not easy to see. I think he was the only one to use it. About a hundred feet out on that trail, there's a little opening with a big stump right in the middle. He used to go out there in the morning. Take a cup a coffee and the letters from Sadie and Emily and read them, over and over.

"I saw him doing that once. He didn't see me and I backed away, didn't say anything. And after, I never went that way again. Figured that was his place. Never talked to him about it, but I think he'd like being buried there. Now that he's died, maybe he won't mind if some mornings, when I'm here at the shack, I borrow his stump and remember my friend."

Kentaki, with his hand on Frankie's shoulder, said, "I think that's the perfect place. Never understood white folks and their graveyards. Everyone buried at the same place. Best to find a spot that was important and good. Makes it easier on the spirits and on those who loved him. I'll start digging now. Shovel out back?"

Frankie nodded and Kentaki walked away. As he did, Ten was carrying Willy inside. Kevin rushed over to help and they set him on the table. Willy was not a big man and he fit just fine. Ten cut away his shirt while Kevin got some water boiling and found some clean cloths they could use as rags. Ten was relieved to see the bullet had gone clean through and it looked like it hadn't hit anything important coming in or going out.

Brock and Huck kneeled next to Gus. It was Huck who first saw the knife wound. The blood was dark. It was easy to tell the wound was deep and worse yet, in the chest. Huck whispered over Gus' head, "He got stuck. Bad."

Gus, unable to lift his head, could still speak and said, "I ain't deaf, Huck. I know I got stuck."

Brock said to Huck, "Let's get him inside and see how bad it is. We need to get him fixed up right away."

With what was obviously an effort, Gus shook his head.

"Ain't gonna do any good and we all three know it. Nope, went in too deep. I can feel it inside. If it's all the same to you, think I'd like to sit out here for a while."

Huck started, "Gus, if we don't—"

"Huck, don't matter if you do. Some wounds can't be fixed. No, think I'll just sit here. Kinda always thought I'd die out on the trail. Hell of a lot better than rotting away as an old man. Least I went out fightin'. Mighta took my life, but they couldn't take that away."

Brock asked, "Gus, what can we do? Anything?"

"About my favorite thing in the world was sitting around at sunset watching the day end, hot mug a coffee in my hand. By myself, or with friends, there wasn't nothin' better. Now, I ain't gonna make it till sunset, but I'd still like that coffee and maybe you—and you, Huck—you could sit with me?"

Kevin, who'd been listening through the open window, turned to grab three mugs, tears streaming down his face.

28

BURIALS

While Ten and Kentaki tended to Willy, Brock and Huck continued to sit with Gus. Gus struggled to hold the coffee mug Kevin had brought and his breathing was growing shallower, but he held on. Somehow, through the pain and the loss of blood and knowing he was dying, his voice stayed strong.

"Spent my whole life chasing cattle. Not for everyone. Watched a lot men die over the years. Others quit. Couldn't take it anymore. Days so hot you think you're gonna melt, so cold you can't imagine being warm again. Indians, outlaws, rustlers. Fought 'em all. Lost good men doing it. Too many."

Huck had grown to truly admire Gus in the time he'd known him. It was a chance meeting in Abilene that led to Huck hiring Gus and Gus bringing along all of his men.

Gus said he would deliver the cattle to Montana Territory, but then he'd be heading back to Texas. He never did. Grew to love the Circle CM and he treated the people and the cattle as if they were his own.

Which, to him, they were. Didn't matter who owned them, they were Gus' responsibility and he loved that. They'd drunk together, fought together, lost friends together. Huck couldn't think of a tougher man. He hated to give up.

"Gus, why don't you let us..."

"Huck, you're a good man and I know you'd do anything for me. In the while I've known you, I've come to think of you as a son. Hope you don't mind. You neither, Brock. But I've been doing this long enough to know when a man's not gonna make it. And I'm not gonna make it. No, just let me sit here for a while longer.

"You know, over the years, I loved quite a few women. Thing is, I never loved a single woman. Never found my Sophie or my Sarah. Not sure I was really lookin', or what I woulda done if I'd found her, but I used to wonder. Wondered what'd it be like to have kids, maybe even grand-kids. Go fishin' with 'em. Learn 'em to ride and shoot. Dress up a little girl in frilly dresses and scare off the boys.

"I think I mighta liked that. You boys. You both got that. Good women. Sophie and Sarah. They're both good women. Maybe, if I'd..."

And with that, Gus closed his eyes and was done. He

took with him more than sixty years of memories. Friends, battles and cattle. Victories and defeats. All that was left were the memories he'd created with the men he'd known. Huck gently took the mug from Gus' hand and Brock tipped his hat over his forehead, blocking the sun from the lifeless eyes, eyes that had seen so much.

The two men stood up and met Kevin at the door. Kevin looked at them and shook his head. All he could say was, "Son-of-a-bitch."

Brock nodded and stepped inside, saying as he did, "Ten, he gonna be okay?"

"If I don't kill him, he will be."

Willy started to speak, but Brock stopped him. "Boys, we just lost Gus. Knife wound was bad. He was tough as nails, but it was too much. Frankie, I heard you talking about burying Deke in a little opening in the forest?"

"You did."

"Think it'd be okay if we put Gus there too?"

Frankie took his time before answering. "It would. Deke loved Gus. Gus took him in when Deke had nothing and knew nothing. Just like with me. Took care of us till we could take care of ourselves. Yeah, put 'em together and they can keep each other company."

IT TOOK MOST of the afternoon to dig the two graves and clean up the line shack. Willy was clearly going to be okay, but he would need time to recover. As for the Sioux, the men dragged their bodies to a small cliff and rolled them over the side. As they did, Kevin said, "Woulda buried 'em, but not after what they did to that little girl and her mother. Man fights a battle against another man, that's one thing, but women and children..."

Frankie, Huck, Ten and Brock walked over to the little spot where Kevin and Kentaki had finished burying Gus and Deke. The sun was setting and the light was beautiful. The spot was well protected, but you could see the mountains. Frankie took off his hat and the others did the same. He looked down at the two graves and then said, "I'm sorry, boys, but I ain't got the words. It's too soon."

Every man there understood and no one else stepped forward to say anything. They stood in silence for almost fifteen minutes, each man with his own thoughts. Then, as the sun finally set, they made their way back to the cabin.

They prepared their supper in almost complete silence. Even Willy was quiet. When supper was done and they were cleaning up, Huck found a bottle of whiskey tucked away on the back of a tall shelf. He took it down and found seven mugs, cups and glasses. He poured some in each until the bottle was empty and then handed one to each man, including Willy. Then he spoke.

"Tomorrow we'll be heading back to the ranch. Guess

Ten and Willy will be staying for a couple of days. Let Willy get some strength back and then we'll send a wagon to pick 'em up. When we get back to the ranch, we're gonna be delivering some bad news to some good people. They're gonna be upset, like we would be. Like we are.

"But for tonight, it's just us. We fought together and we won the battle together. We lost two good men. Deke, that was just bad luck. Coulda happened to any one of us. Frankie, really sorry. As for Gus? Kevin told me what happened. I didn't know he died saving me. I'm not surprised. We all know that's what kind of man Gus was. We all know he would have done that for any one of us.

"Thing is, any one of us woulda done the same thing. I don't say that to take away from what Gus did, but instead to point out he made us all better men. Didn't talk much at all but showed us by example. I'd be dead if it wasn't for Gus and not just today. We'll be back at the ranch tomorrow, but for tonight, it's just us.

"So, let's raise a glass to the men we work, live, fight—and die—with."

29

FRANKIE

Two days later, Frankie woke with the sun. He sat up in bed, the blankets wrapped tightly around him to fight off the morning cold. He still wasn't used to having his own room in the bunk house. None of the men were. No one had ever heard of anything like that before, but when the bunk house was built, Sophie had insisted, even when Gus tried to tell her it wasn't necessary.

It was one of the things he was going to miss about the CM, the way they treated their men. He'd been up most of the night and had finally decided that he was going to go to Italy. Losing Deke and Gus had hit him hard, and it hadn't gotten any better the last couple of days.

He kept thinking about how Gus had died alone. True, he had his friends, good friends, men who would have died to protect him. But he didn't have a wife, or kids, or grand-kids. Frankie realized now that he wanted those things. And that he was never going to find them here. He also hated what had happened to Deke. How he'd had to leave his daughter and the woman he should have married.

Frankie had left New York at age fifteen and hadn't been home in the seven years since. He'd had to leave after killing two men. They'd deserved it. They'd killed his brother. As soon as he did it, his father said Frankie had to leave New York. That he would never be safe there again. Frankie hated it, but knew it was true.

His father had given what little money he could spare and Frankie worked his way west. Gus took him in and had been like a father to him, in the same way Deke had been like a brother. Losing both on the same day was too much and he knew it was time to leave.

His father, mother and sister had moved back to Italy, knowing they wouldn't be safe in New York either. Frankie didn't know where in Italy, though he thought they might have gone back to their old hometown. He'd never been, but his father used to tell stories. Because he didn't know, and they didn't know where he was, there had been no contact. But Frankie had made up his mind that he was going to go back to Italy, find his family and maybe find a wife. He wasn't exactly sure how everything was going to work, but he knew he had to leave now or might never leave.

He got dressed and walked over to the main house. Brock and Sophie were sitting on the front porch, as they often did in the early morning hours. Frankie waved hello and walked up the steps.

"Good morning, Brock. Miss Sophie."

They both said hello and could tell he was uncomfortable.

"I got something to tell you and a favor to ask. It ain't easy."

Sophie gestured to one of the chairs. "Frankie, please take a seat."

"Thank you, ma'am, but no. I should stand. I know you're planning on sending the Parker brothers up to the line shack this morning with a wagon to bring Willy back."

Brock said, "We are."

"I'm wondering if it could be me? If I could take the wagon?"

Brock asked, "You want to ride with the Parkers up to the shack?"

"No, sir. Instead of. I'd like to bring it up there by myself. And that's the other thing. I won't be comin' back."

Sophie and Brock were both surprised but stayed quiet so Frankie could continue.

"See, it's time for me to leave. You've been good to me. All of you. Huck. Gus. Everyone. But I gotta find my family and they're all the way in Italy. I just need to do this. I'll bring the wagon up and bring my horse too. When Ten and

Willy head back down, I'll stay up at the shack for a day or so and then start east. If I could pull wages, I'd be real grateful."

Brock stood up and spoke. "Frankie, of course. I'm sorry you'll be leaving us and I'm sorry about what happened at the shack. I left London when I was a little younger than you and came here to find my father. I hope you're life turns out as you deserve and that you have the same good fortune I have. We will miss you. The Parkers have the wagon ready, so I'll let them know. You might want to say any goodbyes and gather up your gear."

Sophie stood up and gave Frankie a hug, having nothing to say. She stepped inside to gather up the pay owed him. It totaled thirty-eight dollars and she slipped an extra one hundred dollars into the envelope. She knew Brock wouldn't care. Though she knew Frankie wouldn't accept it, she also knew that by the time he looked inside the envelope, it would be too late.

FRANKIE REACHED the shack at noon. Ten and Willy took almost no time packing up. After saying goodbye, they left quickly so that they'd be back to the main ranch before sundown.

About an hour before sunset, Frankie took a glass of

bourbon and a cup of coffee and walked over to where his friends were buried. He sat on the stump that Deke had liked so much and watched the sun start to drop behind the mountains.

"Can't believe you're gone, boys. Gus, I don't know what woulda happened if you hadn't taken me in. You had no reason to do so, but you did. You never said so, but I know you loved me. And I never said so, but you know I thought of you as a father. Thing is, I shoulda said so. I'm sorry.

"I've been thinking, you probably died the way you want to. Out on the trail. Riding with your men. Your family. And the last thing you did was save one of them. It's how I'll always remember you Gus and believe me, I will always remember you.

"Deke. Way too young. Shouldn't a happened. I'm leaving in the morning. Going to make my way to Italy and see if I can find my family. Thing is, if you hadn't been killed, maybe I never woulda left. You were always like a brother to me, Deke.

"I'm going to New York before Italy. Still have a little family there and maybe they know where my mother and father are. Even if they don't, I'm still going. I gotta try.

"Thing is, Deke, I'm gonna stop in Dayton, Ohio on my way. I'm gonna track down your little girl and I'm gonna make sure she knows how much her daddy loved her. I'll give her back all the letters she and her mother wrote, so she'll have 'em. I'm also gonna give her that doll you bought in Fort Worth. I found it in your stuff. I know you didn't think I knew, but I saw you a couple a times playing with it. I know you bought it for her and I'll see that she gets it.

"I promise you that."

30

NEW CHAPTERS

Three months had passed since Frankie had left for the line shack. While they didn't know where he was, he was in everyone's prayers. They hoped for a letter and an update soon on how he was and what was happening.

Those who lived in the bunkhouse had developed a new tradition. Every evening, at sunset, one of them would sit in the chair that until his death had been only for Gus. They would have a hot cup of coffee and think of their lost friend. Of Gus and of Deke. It was good for the men to remember and it was good for Gus and Deke to be remembered.

The same thing took place at the line shack. Every new pair of men who settled in for their five-day stay started the first of those days by visiting the gravesites of their fallen friends.

Cisco was up and about. He required the use of a cane to get around, but even the need for that was passing quickly. The pain of having lost Enyeto was nowhere gone, but as Maria moved to within three months of having the baby, they focused on that as much as possible. Pukeheh said she was healthy and strong and that the baby should be too.

Jimmy and Maddie were enjoying married life and the small cabin that Ray and Pukeheh had loaned them. Jimmy and Ray had started on the town. They had laid out the streets and started some of the building. Dario decided that he would like to once again run a general store and the way the town laid out, it was going to be right next door to Ten and Willy's saloon, which they still planned to call Matt's Place.

As he had promised, Mr. Montgomery was extremely helpful. He had purchased as much lumber as Bozeman and Missoula had on hand and had ordered large amounts from Seattle, a town built on timber. He also had six of his men, in shifts of one week each, help with the building. He personally was paying for the courthouse and sheriff's office to be built.

It was a bit of a surprise, but Alex had agreed to be the judge, and Harry, who found he missed it, agreed to be sheriff. Both were building homes in town.

Claude Pierre decided he needed at least one more trip to Abilene and had left two weeks previously. He carried with him a list of people he was to say hello to for Jimmy, Sarah and Harry. He promised to return before the year was out.

Cole Anderson had taken over for Gus. He'd ridden with Gus as his number two for years and did his best to run things the way that Gus would have wanted.

The friendship between the Circle CM and the Square M continued to grow, as did the relationship between Tom and Claire. Tom now spent far more time at the Square M than he did the CM and was learning as much as he could from Walt and Steve Merle. While he missed Huck and everyone at the CM, he couldn't stand to be away from Claire.

Huck, Sarah, Brock and Sophie sat on Huck and Sarah's front porch. They had been having dinner together twice a week, just the four of them, switching between houses. Huck was very pleasantly surprised to find that Sarah had developed quite a talent for cooking, having worked in her father's kitchen in Abilene.

This night was the first night warm enough that they didn't even have to wear light sweaters. Brock and Huck each had a cigar and a glass of bourbon, while Sophie and Sarah enjoyed a glass of sherry, a habit Sophie had picked up back in Dry Springs.

Brock broke the easy silence. "Nice now that things have settled down a bit."

The other three nodded and Sophie said, "Nice? Settled? It is my experience that you don't do well with 'settled.' That you get restless."

Brock looked at his wife as a smile crept across Huck's face. Brock said, "I'm not sure what you mean. I'm fine being settled."

"Nice? Fine? Settled? I don't think so, honey. Doesn't sound much like the man I married."

Brock looked around, confused. He asked, "What's happening here? What don't I know?"

Huck and Sarah laughed as Sophie continued, "The last time Mr. Montgomery placed an order for lumber in Seattle, I asked him to also place an order for two thousand head of cattle. It's time to add to the herd. He told me there are excellent ranches with cattle to sell in the middle of Washington Territory. It's about six hundred miles away, half the distance of a trip to Abilene. Just enough to keep you from going stir crazy."

Brock, incredulous, asks, "You're sending me to the coast to pick up cattle?"

"Not sending so much. Think of it as my gift to you. I asked Mr. Montgomery to arrange to have them all gathered up in three months, so you don't have to leave for two months. It'll give you something to look forward to."

Brock looked away from Sophie and toward his son. "You knew about this?"

"I did. So did Sarah."

"And you'll be coming with me?"

"I will."

"While it's not as far as Abilene, it's still a long trip. Sarah, you sure you're fine with this?"

"Yes, plus it will give Huck plenty of time."

Huck looked at Sarah, confused, and asked, "Plenty of time for what?"

"To be back here before our baby is born."

~ *The End* ~

ALSO BY SCOTT HARRIS

Huck Clemons Westerns

Abilene Ambush

Brock Clemons Westerns

Dry Springs Trilogy

Coyote Courage

Coyote Creek

Coyote Canyon

Grand Canyon Trilogy

Mojave Massacre

Battle on the Plateau

Ambush at Red Rock Canyon

Open Trails Trilogy

Renegades

Return to Dry Springs

Deadly Trails

Last in the Brock Clemons series

Death in Abilene

Companion Short Story Books

Tales From Dry Springs

Tales From the Grand Canyon

Caz: Vigilante Hunter

Slaughter At Buzzards Gulch

Never Shoot A Woman

McKinley Massacre

Fire From Hell

Hell On Devil's Mountain

They Shouldn't A Killed Her

Stagecoach Willy

600 Bloody Miles

Wounded, Hunted & Alone

Death Across Texas

Six Clemons Modern-Day Western

Revenge on the Border

Juan Carlos Must Die

52 Weeks

*52 Weeks * 52 Western Movies*

*52 Weeks * 52 Western Novels*

*52 Weeks * 52 TV Westerns*

500 Word Micro Shorts

The Shot Rang Out

A Dark & Stormy Night

Bourbon & A Good Cigar

Time To Myself

Western Adventures

Grizzly Creek Runs Red

The Last Comanche

Coyote Junction

Plains: Short and Sweet

Once Upon the Plains

Once More Upon the Plains

Back On the Plains

A Novel Journey – Writing Your First Western

Six Gun Pardners – Collection of Father & Son short stories

I Quit - First contemporary novel